# FORT APACHE

Center Point
Large Print

# FORT APACHE

## HUNTER INGRAM

CENTER POINT LARGE PRINT
THORNDIKE, MAINE

This Center Point Large Print edition
is published in the year 2022 by arrangement with
Golden West Inc.



Originally published in the US by Ballantine.

The text of this Large Print edition is unabridged.
In other aspects, this book may vary
from the original edition.
Printed in the United States of America
on permanent paper sourced using
environmentally responsible foresting methods.
Set in 16-point Times New Roman type.

ISBN 978-1-63808-495-2 (hardcover)
ISBN 978-1-63808-499-0 (paperback)

The Library of Congress has cataloged this record
under Library of Congress Control Number: 2022940812

# Chapter 1

The stiffening breeze whipped the torch flames, alternately shadowing and highlighting the faces of some thirty men gathered, tense with attention, around a small, open dusty spot. The flickering light sharpened cheekbones and hollowed cheeks. It also thinned mouths and made eyes glisten. Every now and then, mouths opened to yell approval, or to shout displeasure.

Two gamecocks circled each other in the small enclosure made by the ring of men. Their wings were partially spread, and their shuffling feet raised dust. Their heads were thrust forward, the fierce little yellow eyes never wavered from their opponent.

It had been a brief but bloody fight, the stains showing black on the birds' plumage, evidence of how often each had been hit. The gaffs, needles of steel affixed to the cocks' natural spurs, gave them a longer and more deadly reach. Each set of gaffs had wetly glistening stains of black, and tiny black spots dotted the dust as the gamecocks maneuvered for position. Both of them were near exhaustion, for their beaks were open as they gasped for air. But the fight would end only when one or both of the cocks were dead.

Lieutenant Owen Parnell shook his head in

unconscious disgust. The splash of light and the sound of voices had caught his attention, and he had walked a short distance out of his way to see what was going on. Just a glimpse was enough to tell him what was happening, but seeing Captain Neal Mundane among the crowd held him a moment longer.

Cockfighting was a cruel and brutal sport, but it had its avid following. Owen should have known that Mundane would be one of those followers. The man was an inveterate gambler, and any game of chance on which money would change hands would interest him.

For the life of him, Owen couldn't see what so fascinated men in cockfighting—unless it was the opportunity to gamble on the outcome, plus the violence that was loosed when two cocks faced each other. Either could account for the following, he thought wryly.

Every man here would argue fiercely against Owen's condemnation of their sport. Owen had listened to cockfighting advocates trying to justify their mania. Fighting was bred into these birds, they claimed; deprive them of it, and the gamecocks would sicken and die.

Maybe that was true, Owen reluctantly admitted, he had seen a gamecock fight its own reflection in a mirror until it could no longer stand. But he still thought cockfighting was a sorry excuse for a sport.

The two cocks suddenly bounded off the ground and met head-on in midair. A pair of gaffs made a lightning strike, and a deadly needle drove through a cock's head, its point protruding on the other side. Both birds fell to the ground, the victor trying vainly to extricate its gaff.

That ends it, Owen thought. The vanquished would never get up again.

Half of the crowd roared approval. The remainder of them muttered curses showing their disappointment. Money would change hands now.

Owen glanced at Mundane to see how he had fared. Mundane wasn't a tall man, but he carried himself with an assurance that made him seem taller. The Arizona sun could redden Mundane's complexion, but never tan his skin. He had a lean face, almost cruel in its thinness, particularly when it was in repose. It was an expressive face, showing whatever emotion he felt. And now it showed savage disappointment in the outcome of the contest.

Good, Owen thought with satisfaction at Mundane's evident bad luck. Travis Ulman, standing beside Mundane, jabbed him with an elbow in the ribs. His face was sly as he said something to Mundane. Whatever it was only increased the blackness on Mundane's face.

Owen's dislike of Mundane had started at West Point, and each succeeding contact only intensified Owen's feeling. Mundane had been a senior when Owen entered West Point, and a plebe under a sadistic upperclassman knew a life of pure hell. Mundane's graduation ended that torture, but the fates must have had it in for Owen, for he had been sent to the Department of Arizona after his graduation. His mouth dropped a foot when he rode onto Fort Bowie to report for his new assignment: the first man he saw was Mundane. Seeing the man was bad enough, but to further embitter the taste in Owen's mouth, he saw that Mundane had been promoted to first lieutenant. A promotion in three years was extraordinarily fast; Owen had never heard of its happening before. He was sure he could hear the fates laughing sardonically. But those fates must have relented, for as it turned out he had not been assigned to duty under Mundane. Mundane was assigned to Fort Lowell, nearer Tucson, and was at Bowie only on an errand.

Owen was a little ashamed of his feelings, imagining himself a childish and vindictive person. Every time he saw Mundane, he felt his resentment rise. Yet he wasn't the only one who felt that way. Mundane's latest promotion had come through just a few weeks ago. Every officer who knew of it felt as bitter as Owen did. Two promotions in seven years was more than anybody could be expected to swallow. A rough, sarcastic joke ran around Fort Bowie: "If you're going to be an officer in the United States Army, forget about doing your job. Just be sure your father is a senator." Officers had a right to that bitter, ironic humor. At the rate Mundane was going he would be a general before he was forty.

Two Mexicans, detaching themselves from the crowd, caught Owen's attention. They owned or handled the gamecocks, for they moved to the center of the ring and bent over the two chickens. The owner of the winning cock had to use force to extract the gaff. The other owner picked up his limp bird and placed its head in his mouth. He sucked hard on it. When he removed the head from his mouth the feathers on the cock glistened with moisture from his mouth. A thin streak of blood ran down from a lip corner.

Owen had never seen this before. He felt a new surge of revulsion. What good would that do to a dead gamecock? His eyes widened. He couldn't believe what he was seeing. The seemingly dead bird was stirring, and light was returning to those glazed eyes. The bird's handler set it on its feet and ran his hands up under its wings and gently shook the chicken. He released it. Owen was sure the cock would fall. But the cock took several wobbly steps. With each step new strength seemed to flow into it.

"I don't believe it," Owen burst out.

The Mexican standing beside him laughed

merrily, the soft, liquid eyes gleaming in the torchlight. "So the lieutenant does not think it is possible for a dead fighting cock to return to life and fight again?"

Owen's Spanish was anything but polished, but he could keep up with the ordinary needs of a conversation. The Mexican women caused him the most trouble. They spit out their words so rapidly that the words became a meaningless jumble of sound.

"It isn't possible," Owen said. "That gaff went clear through his head."

The Mexican nodded agreement. "The lieutenant is right. By all rights the bird should be dead. Sucking on the wound closed it. I do not know how or why it happens. Perhaps the sucking seals the wound and the blood remains in the cock's head instead of dripping out. I only know I have seen it many times. A dead bird gets to its feet, fights again, and sometimes wins. It could happen now."

Mundane whooped with elation at the gamecock's growing steadiness. He wasn't a loser yet.

"You lucky bastard," Owen muttered.

The Mexican glanced questioningly at him. Owen spoke in English and in a voice too low for the Mexican to understand. He didn't try to explain.

The two handlers put their birds beak to beak, and each struggled to get at the other. The men released the cocks and quickly retreated. Before they took a full step, the gamecocks hit each other with a new excess of fury.

It was over in the space of a long breath. Feathers flew, and one of the birds was down. Owen shook his head in disbelief. The victor had turned into the vanquished, for the one left on its feet had a gaff through its head only a moment ago.

The downed cock tried to regain its feet, but its struggles were futile. One of its legs jerked convulsively, then the bird was still. It died in a hurry. Owen guessed that one of those pointed needles had reached the cock's heart.

The victor stood on the dead body, pecked at it several times, then threw back its head and crowed. It took a half-dozen steps. Owen would swear there was a swagger to its walk. All at once, it collapsed as though both legs had been kicked from under it. There was no doubt about its being dead this time.

The triumphant yelling and the bitter cursing was as fully sustained as before—only reversed. In the space of a few breaths, the winners had become the losers.

The gloating on Mundane's face made Owen want to swear. Typical Mundane luck! He seemed to win in everything he touched.

Owen stayed long enough to see Ulman count out money into Mundane's hands. He couldn't see the denominations of the bills, but by the number of them, it had to be a considerable sum.

"You lucky bastard," Owen said again under his breath.

Mundane threw an arm about Ulman's shoulders, said something, then laughed. Ulman shrugged off Mundane's arm and smiled sourly. He was a short, blocky man, dressed in the finest clothes money could buy. He had a prominent, hooked nose, and a thin slash of a mouth. Owen knew Travis Ulman by sight and reputation. Neither endeared the man to him. Ulman was one of the Tucson Ring, comprised mainly of the merchants and contractors who made their money by selling supplies to the Army posts and the Indian reservations. The Army and the Apaches both complained of the quality and quantity of the supplies they received. The Tucson Ring screamed to high heaven about getting the Apaches out of Arizona, but that was only for the public's ears. The Ring knew that if the Apaches were ever sent out of the Territory, the Army would soon follow, or its numbers would be drastically reduced. If that ever happened, the Ring's source of quick and easy profits would dry up.

"That damn Mundane," Owen said in rueful resignation. Mundane knew which crowd to run with. He associated with money. Some of it was bound to rub off on him.

Two new gamecocks were being prepared to be turned loose in the ring. Ulman said something to Mundane. Mundane answered him with a nod.

Another bet, Owen thought. He hoped this time Mundane's luck turned bad.

Owen turned to go, and the Mexican said, "It is not over, Señor. There are many more contests."

"Fine," Owen said and smiled. He hoped Mundane's gambling fever would hold him here until the last fight was over. Maybe that would keep him from seeing Stella Tydings tonight.

The Mexican shook his head, his face perplexed. How could one leave when so much excitement lay ahead?

# Chapter 2

Behind him, Owen heard the excited roar of the small crowd. Another cockfight had started. He grimaced at the ignominious end of the other two chickens. Their bodies were tossed into the crowd, where willing hands grabbed for them. Those two gamecocks would wind up in stews tomorrow.

Owen was better than six feet tall, lean and as durable as a strip of rawhide. The pitiless Arizona sun had blackened his complexion until he could pass for one of the natives, except for his clothing and the intense blue eyes. He was thick through the shoulders and thin in the flanks. Long hours in the saddle had whittled away the last unnecessary ounce of flesh. He wasn't handsome in any sense. His features were cut with harsh strokes. His nose was long and aquiline, the mouth on a too generous scale. He displayed flashing, even teeth when he laughed, and that happened often, for he had a quick sense of humor and a wit to match. His step was quick and light, and he gave the impression of strong, controlled vitality. Women sensed that, and it appealed to them.

His pulse quickened as he thought of Stella. His pick of the single women in Tucson was almost unlimited, for he was aware of the thinly veiled invitation in too many eyes. But he was interested in only one pair. Damn it! Wasn't it always that way?

Stella Tydings was tall for a woman, the crown of her lustrous black hair reaching to the bridge of his nose. He had been enthralled with her from their first meeting. Her smile started with the slow crinkling of her eye corners, then spread slowly over her face, until her lips were widely parted with it. He grimaced as he recalled the vow he made after first seeing her. He would capture her once and for all. So far, he had made little headway.

Was his intense dislike of Mundane due to the fact that Stella displayed just the opposite of his feeling for the captain? Owen grinned wryly as he remembered that their three quarrels had been over the interest she showed in Captain Neal Mundane. Those quarrels had been hot and heavy. She claimed his jealousy blinded him; she denied all his allegations that she treated Mundane with far more consideration than she did him. When she was angry, her eyes chilled until they could freeze him. Three times, he had stalked away, swearing he would never return. But he always had. It was either that, or be thoroughly miserable.

How sweet and warm the making-up of those quarrels had been. She pointed out that she treated all her male acquaintances the same, that her warm smile and bubbling eagerness of spirit misled them. Owen guessed the explanation was true—eagerness made each damn fool think he was the special one. Maybe you're one of the fools, he thought, and the sour smile returned to his mouth.

He had to believe he was more important to her than all the others, but still that miserable little doubt remained to gnaw on him. She was elusive as a handful of smoke. Every time he was sure his fingers could close on her, she slipped deftly away, leaving him frustrated and empty-handed.

"Maybe it's Mundane's rank that earns all that consideration from Stella," he reflected aloud, then snorted at the ridiculousness of the thought. It wouldn't have made any difference to Stella if Mundane had stars all over his shoulders. She wasn't the kind of a woman who let money or importance cloud her thinking. The last quarrel had been perilously close to a permanent split between them. Owen had foolishly suggested that Mundane's bars must be looming big in her eyes, and he winced as he remembered the blazing eyes that cut him down. Stella had called him an immature child, and she might have been right. She pointed out that Mundane's rank made no difference to her; Mundane had consideration for others, easy wit and charm. Those were the only things important to her. She would treat Mundane the same whether he was a private or a general.

Owen had wilted before her anger. Stella felt she was right about Mundane, but Owen knew she was wrong. Mundane had a superficial charm that was rarely displayed unless he wanted something. As for consideration for others, all Stella had to do was to talk to some of the men under Mundane. That would change her opinion in a hurry.

Owen had wisely kept his mouth shut. Anything he said in a moment like this would be attributed to temper and jealousy. He wasn't going to get anywhere with her by handling her the way he had been doing.

"Okay, Stella," he said. "Your way." He would have to wait for Stella to discover for herself the true man beneath Mundane's false exterior. Owen squirmed at the length of time that would take, but he knew of no way to shorten it.

He realized he had been speaking aloud when a passerby turned his head to stare back at him.

Owen grinned sheepishly. Army men had a bad enough standing with the people of Tucson without him adding to it by making them think he was touched.

Tucson showed evidence of its growing prosperity. Owen visited it as often as his duties would permit, which was far too rare. The townspeople bragged that Tucson had a population of over three thousand, with more people pouring in every day. The latter part of that boast was probably exaggerated, but it would remain partially true as long as the Apache menace was contained. The Apaches were on the reservation now, and Owen prayed with all the fervor in his soul they would remain there. He couldn't begin to estimate how many hot desert miles he had covered in helping to herd the Apaches onto their reservation. That was an accomplishment of magnitude, and the Army still shuddered as it remembered how many years it had taken and how many lives it cost.

Civilians raved and ranted at the bloodthirstiness of the red devils, and perhaps from their viewpoint, Owen would feel the same. But he did not have a crazed hatred for the Apaches. He had fought them long enough to learn to respect them. The civilians couldn't or wouldn't see that the Apaches were fighting for their own land—for their very way of life. Yes, Owen had earned an understanding of the Apaches. They were incredibly tough: small, wily people with a durability that was appalling to the white mentality. Owen did not treat them with disdain or contempt as too many officers did.

The Army lived in constant fear of a breakout. It needed only a small band out of control to send chills of apprehension up and down the Army's spine. Just a handful of renegades, led by one competent leader, could throw a pall of panic over the entire Territory of Arizona. Owen scowled, thinking of how impossibly difficult it was to dig a handful of Apaches out of the vast reaches of this desert and mountain country. That small band of renegades could scatter like a startled covey of quail to reassemble later. Then, instead of following a single trail, the Army had two dozen trails or more.

The Apaches would raid and loot and burn. Always the victims were the defenseless farmers or ranchers caught in the Apaches' path. How the newspapers loved that: each raid put new life into their front pages. The Tucson Ring would yell loud enough to be heard in Washington, demanding more soldiers to protect Arizona citizens. Eastern newspapers would seize on the first reports and blow them out of all proportion. The president would threaten Congress for being lax, and Congress, indignant over the fact that law and order couldn't be maintained in Arizona, would rave at the Army, pointing out how much money had been spent on the Apache problem with no visible results. Every Army Officer in Arizona, during these frantic periods, would reach up every so often to see if his head still remained on his shoulders—the president and Congress were in a headhunting mood; God help the officer who made a mistake, or what Congress considered to be one.

Owen grimaced. When the brass walked on eggs, the tremors running through them reached down into every officer under their command. It would be pure hell. Meanwhile, the weather seemed to grow hotter, horses and mules were in vile moods, ready to kick the living hell out of anybody who was careless around them. Men were tight-tempered. If they talked at all, it was in moody words, and their eyes moved constantly as though they tried to see in all directions at once.

There had been no outbreaks for several months, but one was building up. Owen sensed subtle little indications of unrest in the Apaches on the reservations. It was like the lull before a bad storm when the air was too oppressive, too still. A man sweated and endured until the storm broke, easing the oppressive feeling.

There was nothing definite that Owen could point to and say, "It's going to blow up there." Right now, all he had to go on was a crawling sensation between his shoulder blades. Apache complaints about the quantity and quality of food were steadily mounting, particularly on the San Carlos Reservation. The young warriors there were hot-eyed and sullen. Too many small groups of the Apaches had broken up their talk at Owen's approach and stalked away, or stared coldly through him.

Owen sighed. Those black eyes were knives, stabbing clear through a man. He could truthfully say he had worked hard to earn the Apaches' trust. He had never lied or broken a promise to them. All that hard work could be thrown away in an instant. The sad trouble was that too many whites were not concerned enough to find out what was bothering the Apache.

Owen quickened his pace. He wanted to empty his mind of all this worry, particularly when he was going to see Stella. He smiled ruefully, wondering if he could keep his troubles hidden from her perceptive eyes.

Now and then, some of the populace nodded or spoke to him as they passed. But those people were in the decided minority. Owen wore an Army uniform, and in too many cases it only earned him suspicion and scorn.

Yet the longer he stayed in Arizona, the more he liked the country. How well he recalled his first shuddering contemplation of a vast, lonely country, bathed in heat and filled with hardships. That feeling was all gone now. The lonely reaches were still here, though the frightening aspect had vanished. Owen now looked at this vast empty land with a new eye. He saw a brooding grandeur that soothed a man, if he would let it, and yes, even filled his soul with peace. How many nights had he lain awake fumbling to express what he felt about this land? He never quite reached what he wanted to express, but it no longer mattered.

Tucson wasn't as imposing as the surrounding countryside. He thought he knew the reason and smiled crookedly. Tucson was filled with people, and people always took something from nature.

The town was built upon a low ridge, slanting to the valley floor. A large portion of Tucson straggled along the banks of the twisting Rio Santa Cruz. Most of the year it was a slow, muddy stream, though a couple of times Owen had seen it in flood. In this hot land even that muddy water was beckoning. Tucson's history went back to a time when only Indians lived here. Later most of its population was made up by people of Spanish and Mexican descent. The coming of the Americans had changed everything. Tucson was no longer a somnolent town, drowsing in the sun.

Owen couldn't say he actually disapproved of the change in Tucson, but something about its progress put an unease in him that he couldn't quite name. Maybe the progress was too fast. There was never a moment to rest, to contemplate upon what had been built, to see if that building was good. Maybe it was the false set of values that placed the American dollar above all else. He chuckled wryly. How the Tucson Ring would hoot if they heard the latter.

The town was surrounded by fields of grain and fine fruit orchards. The tall cottonwood trees along the river added to the splashes of green that broke up the monotony of the desert.

The adobe buildings were mostly shades of brown and gray, though a few daring individuals were beginning to break up that pattern by using different colors. Tucson had once been a walled town, but the town had grown so much that long ago it spilled out from behind the original protection against marauders. The arid streets of the old and new sections were alike, covered by a fine, powdery dust. Each passing foot and hoof stirred the dust until it rose in a haze that filled one's nostrils and covered his clothing. Day and night, traffic always moved on the streets.

Owen turned his head as he heard the rapid clop-clop of hoofs. Even as loud as that noise was, the dolorous squeaking of wheels penetrated through the beat of the hoofs, setting Owen's teeth on edge. Six teams of mules drew the wagon, and by the strain in their bodies, Owen would bet the wagon was overloaded. The mule-skinner stood in the box and lashed the teams, trying to force additional effort from them.

Owen choked back an oath as the thin cloud of dust rose in the air and settled all over him. The dust didn't irritate him as much as the driver beating animals that were already giving all they could. That crazy need of haste seemed to be an ingrained American trait. He thought cynically that the haste was probably explained by the need to squeeze a few more dollars into the twenty-four hours of a day.

He watched the wagon and mules until they turned out of sight. Quickening his pace he turned onto Calle Real. The coming of the Americans brought change to everything, even to renaming the old streets. This one was now called Main Street by the Americans. Owen preferred the old name. Calle Real had a softer, more liquid sound.

He passed Charley Brown's Congress Hall, the best saloon in town. While Brown didn't like soldier business much more than the other saloons in town, he still didn't refuse to serve soldiers. At times, his service could be insultingly slow, but he didn't try to palm off the worse rotgut as other saloons did. Another thing to his credit—Owen hadn't heard of Brown cheating a soldier.

As Owen passed the saloon, a half-dozen soldiers entered the building. It was payday, and Fort Lowell was only a few miles out of town. Every soldier who could get a pass would be itching to spend the money in his pockets. Happy headaches, Owen thought sardonically. He couldn't blame the enlisted men for seeking a few moments of oblivion from the bad quarters, the not much better food, and the unceasing monotony.

Those six soldiers were wise in picking Brown's saloon. While they might not be welcome, they wouldn't be openly insulted, either. They wouldn't have to listen to thinly veiled civilian remarks about the Army being a bunch of do-nothings living off tax dollars—or even better, of being Apache-lovers . . . Owen's lips curled. According to the civilian version, the only way to protect the Territory was to kill or run out every Apache, man, woman, and child. That was the way they talked when everything was peaceful. But the moment hostilities broke out, they ran screaming to the Army for protection quick enough.

All up and down the street, Mexican males slouched or sat against the buildings. Owen had long ago decided they were a friendly race, their liquid brown eyes gentle and anxious. But they were afraid of the Americans, never sure how that volatile temper would break. These men wore loose trousers of coarse white cloth, and scrapes hung from their shoulders. The serape was a useful garment with a head-hole in its center. When the weather was too chilly it made a personal tent with only the head showing. They would sit or slouch like this, chattering incessantly until the increasing evening's chill drove them inside. They smoked an inordinate number of hand-rolled cigarritos, and the ground around them was littered with butts.

Owen had often wondered how the Mexicans existed, for there didn't seem to be an over-abundance of ambition in many of them. A few of them kept small stores called tendajons. They sold small black cakes of sugar, carne sece—dried beef jerked and dried in the sun—and strings of hot, dried red chili peppers that would take off an incautious man's head.

In a way, Owen envied these people. They weren't going anyplace, but none of them worried about it. They would never have the material things that were so important to Americans. It seemed as though all they needed to keep them happy was a few sacksful of cheap tobacco, enough clothing to cover them, copious quantities of the inexpensive native beer, and an occasional drink of mescal or tequila. As for mañana, it would take care of itself.

Owen wouldn't say these people had the right idea. But they wouldn't be scourged by the whip of dissatisfaction, either.

He turned at the next corner, heading for an alley that would be a shortcut to Stella's house. The alley ran behind several saloons, and he proceeded carefully. Even with full moonlight, the shadows were always thick and black here. A careless foot could tread on a tin can and turn an ankle.

His nose wrinkled at the smell. A lot of garbage was dumped along this alley. Maybe the distance he would save wasn't worth enduring this stench.

A cat disturbed at its feeding spat at him, defiantly standing its ground. Those bigger, scurrying flashes of motion could be nothing but rats. The cat wasn't interested in them—why should it be, when so much easier feeding was abundantly at hand?

A dark blob of shadow, a dozen yards ahead and close to the ground, caught Owen's attention. It had the shape and proportion of a human figure. Probably some drunk had wandered back here to sleep off his overload of liquor.

Owen cautiously approached the shadow. There was no telling what he might stumble across in this alley.

He cursed softly as he neared the figure. That was a soldier stretched out on the ground. His cheeks tightened as he turned the unconscious form over. Owen knew this one. Trooper Mulvaney was a good soldier. Mulvaney always confined his drinking to payday, and Owen had never known him to drink himself unconscious.

He prodded Mulvaney with a boot toe. "Come on, Mulvaney," he said roughly. "Snap out of it."

His anger grew at the lack of response from Mulvaney. This was the kind of thing that put the Army into a bad light with the civilians.

He prodded Mulvaney harder. "Get up, Mulvaney." If he had to, he would kick Mulvaney back onto his feet.

# Chapter 3

Something got through to Mulvaney's befogged senses, for he stirred and groaned. His eyes opened, and he stared bewilderedly at Owen.

"Get up," Owen said in quiet anger. "You're a disgrace to that uniform."

Mulvaney managed to sit up, but it took tremendous effort. He stared at Owen as though he had never seen him before.

"Oh, God," he moaned. "I'm sick."

He proved it by vomiting, soiling the front of his uniform.

Owen stepped back in disgust. He felt no sympathy at all for Mulvaney. Mulvaney had overestimated his capacity tonight. He had wallowed like a hog in cheap rotgut.

"Get up, Mulvaney," Owen repeated. "If you disobey, it'll cost you some time in the guardhouse."

Mulvaney tried to obey the command but couldn't. He made a feeble effort to get to his feet and failed. He peered foggily up into Owen's face. "I can't make it, Lieutenant. Honest, I'm sick."

Owen moved in close enough to catch a good whiff of the stain on Mulvaney's uniform. The stench was nauseating, comprised of the odor of whisky, stomach content, and something else he couldn't quite place. The latter smell had a sweetish, sickening quality, reminding Owen of some kind of medicine. Maybe Mulvaney wasn't lying.

"How many drinks did you have, Mulvaney?"

Mulvaney supported his head in his hands. "Just one," he mumbled.

Owen snorted.

Mulvaney caught the skepticism in the snort, for he said earnestly, "That's all, Lieutenant. I stopped in Tribollet's saloon, and I remember ordering one drink. It tasted funny, but I got it down. That's all I remember until I came to out here."

Mulvaney's words rang true. The rear door of Tribollet's saloon was a half block down the alley. But Mulvaney could have been carried out and dumped here.

Owen's jaw hardened. Tribollet was notorious for his crooked games and rotten whisky. Owen had heard too many reports of Tribollet drugging a soldier's drink, particularly on payday. Then it was a simple matter for the women who worked for him to dig their greedy fingers into an unconscious soldier's pockets.

"Did you get paid today?" Owen asked.

"Sure. That's why I rode into town. I got my pass and—"

Owen cut him short. "Who was with you?"

Mulvaney shook his head. "I came in alone."

"Who saw you in Tribollet's?"

Mulvaney had to puzzle over that question. "Flora did. I offered to buy her a drink. I was talking to her, then everything faded away."

Owen nodded grimly. He didn't know who this Flora was, but she shouldn't be hard to find.

"How much money have you got left?"

Mulvaney fumbled through his pockets, and his face loosened with shock. "Not a damned cent. The bastards took everything I had."

"You knew better than to go in there," Owen said unfeelingly. Tribollet's reputation was enough to warn off any soldier. Tribollet was supposed to be a member of the Tucson Ring, making all the profit he could off the Army and the Apaches.

He reached down to give Mulvaney a hand. "Come on. Get on your feet."

"Where you taking me, Lieutenant?" Mulvaney asked apprehensively.

"To a doctor's to see if we can get you straightened out."

With Owen's aid, Mulvaney got his feet under him. "Oh, God," he moaned. "My legs are string."

"Start walking," Owen snapped. "You'll make it."

Mulvaney was a short, stocky man, and his weight bore heavily on Owen. His first few steps were faltering and unsure, but they strengthened. By the time they reached the end of the alley, he could walk without Owen's assistance.

"I'm going back there and clean those bastards out," he said wrathfully.

"You'll do nothing of the sort," Owen snapped. "Did they empty your head, too?"

"If you think I'm going to stand for them robbing me—" Mulvaney started indignantly.

Owen's face was a hard mask. "You'll do what the doctor says. I'll take care of the other matter for you."

Mulvaney looked at Owen's expression and subsided. But he muttered all the way to Dr. Haines's office.

Owen thought of Stella and sighed. Everything seemed to be working to prevent him from seeing her tonight.

Dr. Haines looked up from his desk as they entered. He was a crusty man with a face that was beginning to erode without softening. Haines's manner was gruff and at times he had an acid tongue, but his hands were gentle. Owen had observed him handling the sick and hurt before, and had come to the conclusion that hard exterior was a protection to cover his inner softness.

"What have you got, Lieutenant?" Those faded, old eyes swept over Mulvaney. "From the looks of him I'd say another drunk."

Owen smiled bleakly. "Get closer to him, then tell me what you think."

"I've smelled drunks before," Haines said querulously.

"Maybe not like this one. He says he had one drink in Tribollet's. Mulvaney's not a liar."

"Ah," Haines said. He got up and moved close to Mulvaney and bent over him. His nose wrinkled at what he smelled.

"So you recognize it," Owen said.

"I do," Haines said dryly. "I've smelled it before."

"Tell me what he had beside whisky."

"Laudanum," Haines said promptly. "Tincture of opium. A few drops in a man's drink makes him sicker than a dog and completely helpless."

"Mulvaney was both," Owen said. His eyes were beginning to darken. They always did when he was thoroughly angry.

"If he was at Tribollet's, he was robbed, Lieutenant."

"He was that," Owen said grimly.

Indignation swept across Haines's face. "When is the Army going to get smart enough to order its soldiers to stay out of Tribollet's?"

Owens shrugged. "That's up to higher rank. But I'm going to do my little bit about it right now."

"Don't just storm in there and start raising hell," Haines advised. "Tribollet keeps a couple of rough floormen on duty at all times. He won't take any criticism."

"I'll keep that in mind," Owen said quietly.

He started for the door, and Mulvaney took a couple of wobbly steps after him.

"Wait for me, Lieutenant. I'm going, too." Mulvaney swayed, then threw out a hand to a chair to steady himself. He looked like a hollow-legged man. That usually florid face now had a definite green cast.

"You're going no place," Owen said sharply. "Doc, can you do anything for him?"

"Not much. I'll give him something for his stomach. About all he can do is to lie down until it passes."

Owen nodded. "That'll do." He walked out the door, his hands clenched so tightly they ached. So Tribollet had a couple of rough floormen. He wasn't going to bust into Tribollet's by himself and wind up where Mulvaney had been.

Owen stopped outside the doctor's office, trying to think of just how he was going to handle Tribollet. He knew he would get no place by going in there alone.

His face brightened as four soldiers came down the street toward him. They had been in town long enough to be in a high, good mood, for they were singing.

Owen stopped them, waving away the uneasiness that touched their faces at his appearance.

"I've got a job for you," he said crisply. He told them what had happened to Mulvaney, and they listened attentively.

"Tribollet's been getting away with that too long," Owen said. "We won't get Mulvaney's money back, but maybe we can collect something out of Tribollet's hide."

Four faces glowed with unholy delight. "You just lead the way, Lieutenant."

Owen checked them just inside Tribollet's door. "Wait here until I call for you." He was quite sure there would be a brawl; he was going to make sure of that.

A woman stopped him as he approached the bar. She wasn't old in years, but she had a burden on her spirit that drained her, making her seem far older than she was.

"I'm looking for Flora," he said pleasantly.

"I can do more for you than she can," she wheedled.

Owen shook his head. "It has to be Flora."

Her eyes looked like an angry cat's. For a moment, he was sure she was going to spit at him. "She's at the far end of the bar," she said sullenly, and flounced away.

Owen approached Flora. Mulvaney didn't have any more taste in selecting women than he did in picking saloons. Flora was a faded blonde, getting too plump. She had lived too hard, too fast, and the shadow of that living was in her eyes.

"Flora?" Owen asked.

Her face brightened. "Why yes, Lieutenant." Her eagerness showed she was pleased in the improvement on the caliber of her usual customers. "What can I do for you?"

"You can tell me how much you stole out of Mulvaney's pockets. You drugged his drink."

That startled flicker in her eyes was pure fright. Her mouth opened under the shock of his accusation, and her face looked vapid.

She struggled with her thoughts, unable to get them in coherent order, then she spluttered, "Are you crazy? I don't know what you're talking about."

Owen stared levelly at her. She knew what he was talking about. Those first reactions had betrayed her. "You know, all right," he murmured.

Her eyes narrowed and filled with a malevolent gleam. At the moment, she was almost a twin of the first woman who had stopped Owen. It was odd how much such women looked alike when they were crossed.

"Get away from me," she hissed. Her voice raised, and she called shrilly, "Bob, this damned lieutenant is giving me trouble."

Bob Tribollet came around the end of the bar, his face hard. He was a lean man, and he hadn't shaved or changed his shirt in the past week. A long scar showed through the beard stubble on his jaw. He grinned mockingly, displaying bad teeth.

"Is he bothering you, Flora?"

Her cackle was meant to be a laugh. "He sure as hell is. He's accusing me of something I don't know anything about. Did you ever hear of a soldier called Mulvaney?"

There was amusement in the look exchanged between Tribollet and Flora. Both of them were familiar with that name.

"Stranger to me," Tribollet drawled.

Tribollet's backing made Flora more sure of herself. "He even accused me of drugging that soldier's drink."

There was no semblance of amusement in Tribollet's eyes now. "Get your ass out of here, Lieutenant. Now! Before you're really sorry!"

"As sorry as Mulvaney was? You"—Owen's contemptuous eyes raked Flora—"or this woman stripped him of every cent he had, then dumped him out in the alley. You've been getting away with that for a long time, haven't you, Tribollet? Maybe it's about over—"

"Why, goddamn you," Tribollet said thickly. "You can't come in here spewing lies like that. I'll teach you—"

He sprang forward, swinging a wild fist.

Owen had been waiting for such a move. He ducked the blow and glided inside Tribollet's reach. He hit Tribollet flush on the nose. His knuckles landed higher than he wanted, but it was still a good, solid blow. Tribollet went over backwards, a startled squawk jerked out of him.

He landed on his back, and for a moment his eyes were bleary with the sudden rush of pain. Blood spurted out of his nose, running like a filled keg with its bung knocked out. It poured over his chin and ran down on his shirt. He wiped the back of his hand across his injured nose, smearing blood all over his face.

Tribollet lay there, shaking his head, trying to regroup his scattered senses. His eyes cleared, and he looked up at Owen with more hatred in his eyes than Owen had ever seen before.

Owen waited, easy and relaxed, curious to see how this would go. Would Tribollet push it farther, or let the matter drop?

Tribollet opened his mouth and bawled, "Hade! Celso! Where the hell are you?" He kept screaming those names, the fury mounting in his voice.

Two big men hurried into the room from a side door. They had bulk but little else. Their eyes were dull, and they moved ponderously. They looked with shock at the bleeding man on the floor.

"Jesus, boss! What happened to you?"

Tribollet cursed them with every oath at his command. "What the hell do I hire you for? If you're not around when I need you—" He was choking on his own spleen, and he stopped for breath.

"We just stepped out for a breath of air," one of the big men said uneasily. "Just tell us what you want us to do."

"I want that lieutenant roughed up real good," Tribollet said in a rasping tone. "I mean real good. Then throw him out."

The two big men whipped about to face Owen, and he saw the wicked anticipation fill their eyes. He raised his hand and beckoned to the four soldiers standing near the front door. Maybe he had waited a little too long.

Hade and Celso lumbered toward Owen, their fists bunched.

Owen watched them with calculating eyes. These two had probably carried Mulvaney out into the alley and dumped him. The two were splitting to come at him from opposite sides to get at him. This was an old story, and from long experience they were positive of how it would turn out.

Owen decided on the one on his left. He whirled and took him full on, grunting with pleasure as he sank his fist up to his wrist into the soft belly. The breath whooshed out of the man, and he doubled over, his complexion turning green. He wrapped his arms about his stomach, his mouth wide as he gasped for air.

Owen spun to meet the other one. The second floorman moved faster than Owen thought he could. Owen didn't fully complete his turn. That clubbing blow smashed him across the side of his neck, the brutal force knocking him backward against the bar. He clung to the bar to keep from going down. Now Owen was sure he should have called in the four soldiers sooner.

He tightened his grip on the edge of the bar, trying to shake the blackness that threatened to envelop him. Vaguely, he heard Flora scream, then there was the rush of booted feet.

A blow smashed him in the face. That should have triggered the blackness into taking him, but he still refused to go down. He kept shaking his head, trying to get the ringing out of it. What was holding back the third blow? Yelling laced with curses and grunts of pain seemed to have broken out all around him. Dimly in the background, he thought he heard the breaking of furniture.

An arm went about his shoulders, and he tried to gather enough strength to shake it off.

"You all right, Lieutenant?" a solicitous voice asked.

Owen blinked his eyes several times to clear them. He smiled weakly as he looked into a soldier's worried face.

"Just fine," he said, trying to keep the lie from showing too much in his voice.

"How far shall we go?" the soldier asked.

It took a moment for Owen to understand what the soldier meant. He grinned as it came to him. "Not too gently, soldier. They've robbed enough soldiers to pay for whatever damage you might do."

The soldier whooped his delight and sprang back into the fray.

The floormen were rough, but the soldiers were rougher; they also had the odds with them. The soldiers split, a pair to work on each floorman. The one Owen hit in the belly was the first to go down. One of the soldiers put a boot into his ribs, and the toughness quickly seeped out of him. He rolled over on his face, covered his head with his arms, and stayed there.

Owen's head cleared rapidly, and he began to enjoy this. Chance had let him pick four good men. One of them went down and bounded to his feet like a rubber ball, charging back into the melee. Nobody could question that one's stamina. His face blazed with pure pleasure, as he swung another blow at the floorman still remaining on his feet.

Owen glanced at Flora. She was screaming her lungs out. He kept an eye on Tribollet, who was just getting on his feet. His face was maniacal, a mixture of rage and fear. The customers had bunched near the door, keeping as far as they could from this madhouse.

The second floorman was rocking under a barrage of blows. The soldiers swarmed him from all sides, and no matter which way he turned, he couldn't protect himself. He went down; he wasn't out, but he was bleeding badly. He looked up foggily at the ring of faces hanging over him, made a wise evaluation of the situation, and decided to stay where he was.

Tribollet wasn't that smart. He seized a chair by its back and rushed the soldiers.

Owen demanded a lot of his rubbery legs. He forced them to move in a hurry, and he got to the man just as Tribollet lifted the chair to crash it down on an unsuspecting head.

Owen grabbed the chair and jerked it out of Tribollet's hands. Tossing the chair aside, Owen smashed Tribollet in the ear. He followed it up with a series of blows, beating Tribollet across the floor.

Tribollet sagged visibly. Owen kept him from falling with his last two punches. He hit him once more and stepped back to let him fall. Tribollet's face was a gory mess.

Owen reflectively rubbed his knuckles as he looked at that unconscious face. Tribollet would probably have a few new scars to add to the one he already had on his face.

One of the soldiers scooped up the chair Owen had jerked away from Tribollet, hefted it, and glanced questioningly at Owen. Owen guessed what the soldier had in mind and nodded approval.

The soldier made a mighty swing, releasing the chair at its apex. The chair sailed over the bar and smashed against the backbar mirror.

The four soldiers were poised on springs, just waiting for Owen's words to release them. They would have broken this place into small bits.

"I guess that'll do," Owen said regretfully. He looked at Tribollet, then sardonically at Flora. Maybe this had taught those two enough of a lesson to treat a soldier with more respect the next time one came in.

He walked outside with the four men, and they chattered animatedly. This had turned into an evening they would remember quite a while.

"You done all right, sir," one of them said, "after you got started." He pulled a handkerchief out of his pocket and handed it to Owen. "You're doing some bleeding."

Owen knew he was. His lips were split, and they hurt every time he moved them.

He held the handkerchief against his sore mouth and with the other hand pulled what money he had out of his pocket. He handed it to the ranking man, a corporal. "Corporal, enjoy yourselves the rest of the evening. I'd suggest you pick a better place than this one. Try Brown's."

Their faces shone with approval of Owen. "Lieutenant," the corporal said, "the next time you go out for another evening like this, will you let us in on it?"

"I'll keep it in mind," Owen said gravely.

He watched them go down the street. They were singing at the top of their lungs. He hastily stopped his grin before it was full-fledged; his battered lips hurt too much to grin. Damn it, he hadn't even thought to ask those soldiers' names. Probably they came from Fort Lowell. He regretfully shook his head at his lack of consideration, though he guessed it didn't really matter. He had thanked them as effusively as he could.

He turned to continue on to Stella's house. He was in one hell of a shape to be calling on her, but he was still going. His opportunities to see her came too rarely for him to pass up one. He forgot his split lips and grinned at a thought. Maybe his wounds would earn him special attention. Damn it! Those lips hurt.

# Chapter 4

Owen held the handkerchief to his sore mouth as he walked to the Tydings house in the old part of Tucson. By the time he reached the adobe house, the bleeding had stopped, but it had made a mess of his shirt.

He knocked softly on the door. His heart had picked up that familiar increased pace at the prospect of seeing Stella.

The house was built in the old Spanish style, its adobe walls three feet thick and built flush with the street, with no front yard of any kind. Its two windows, very tall and narrow, were covered with a grid of iron bars, perhaps a relic of the old days when house dwellers feared the raids of banditos and Indians. Professor Tydings would know why those windows were so heavily barred, if only Owen could think to ask him. But each time he was here, seeing Stella drove all other thoughts out of his mind.

Stella answered his knock. The shadows prevented her from noticing his bruised face and the bloodstain on his shirt.

She reached out and seized his hand. "Owen." Pleasure was evident in her voice. "I didn't expect you tonight."

"I didn't expect to be here, either," he

answered. "General Crook wanted me to take some dispatches to Fort Lowell. As long as I was that close to Tucson, you didn't think I'd miss an opportunity to see you, did you?"

She drew him inside. Her face was soft, and Owen hoped his words were responsible for that. Her touch was warm, and he wished he could read something far more intimate in her touch. Her eyes were magnificent, and he stared at them with an intensity that forced her to look away. He exulted at that. Maybe he was beginning to reach her. She wasn't quite twenty, but her age wasn't the cause of her being flustered. She was a woman grown and mature in every way. Owen had to believe he was making headway with her.

The turned-down kerosene lamp gave faint illumination inside the front door, but it was enough for Stella to see his marked face and his stained clothing.

"Owen," she gasped. "You've been hurt."

"It looks worse than it is," he said wryly. Briefly, he sketched Mulvaney's experience. "I found four soldiers and went back to that saloon. I felt Mulvaney had a right to some collecting in his favor. It was quite a brawl, but it didn't last long." He didn't name the saloon; he doubted that Stella had even heard of Tribollet's. "Maybe we changed some minds on how to treat soldiers."

Her face darkened as he talked. "Is there much of that going on in Tucson?"

"Too much," he said gravely. "It's hard to stamp out. Too many people in this town will make a dollar any way they can."

Her forefinger lightly touched the corner of his mouth. She was angry about what had happened, for her breathing was rapid. "Let me see what I can do about this."

She led him into the kitchen and poured water from an olla into a pan. She soaked a cloth in the water and gently dabbed at his mouth. "I'm not hurting you?" she asked anxiously.

It hurt a little, but he wouldn't have admitted it for the world. He would take a dozen more such injuries as this just to get similar attention.

She finished cleansing his face and said, "I don't think I can do anything about your shirt."

He smiled, and his mouth didn't hurt as much as before. Maybe her presence had healing power. "I've got another shirt," he said lightly.

She laughed before she said, "Father's in the courtyard. He'll want to hear about this."

Owen thought that Professor Tydings would be interested. Her father was intensely interested in everything that went on in his newly adopted land.

Owen followed Stella to the courtyard. Like most Spanish houses, the courtyard was in the rear of the house. Owen remembered his reaction the first time he had seen this courtyard. It was a little oasis of beauty and contentment. People passing along the street never had the slightest idea it existed.

The small walled-in enclosure was planted with skill and care. Stella had a way with growing things. Owen had commented on it several times. Her shrug disclaimed all credit. She gave the credit to Ramón, the Mexican gardener hired by the Tydingses. Owen didn't voice his skepticism, but he hadn't seen any evidence that Ramón was interested in anything except sitting in the shade. Whatever he did was because of Stella's urging.

Stella could rattle off the name of every shrub, every plant. When it came to that, Owen felt ignorant. He could identify the banana tree in one corner of the courtyard, and he knew that the bright splash of red covering one wall was bougainvillea. But beyond those two plants, he was lost.

Tydings rose from his chair and eagerly welcomed Owen. He was a tall, lean man, but that awful cadaverous look he had had on his arrival was fading. Owen noticed that his handshake was stronger. Tydings was whipping the tuberculosis that sent him to Arizona in the first place. His eyes had a bright new gleam, and that air of discontented brooding was gone. Tydings had given up his position as professor of history at Yale University to try to regain his health. It was small wonder that he had been on the brink of despair: he had given up a familiar home, he had left a country he knew and loved, and six months before he left for Arizona, his wife had died. Owen had a deep respect for Tydings. This man had a strong inner spirit to make the comeback he did.

Tydings didn't notice Owen's bruised mouth nor his bloodstained shirt until he dropped his hand.

He whistled softly, and his eyes were keen as he observed the damage. "You've had some trouble," he stated.

"You might put it like that," Owen admitted.

"He's been playing little-boy games," Stella said tartly. "He's been fighting."

Owen looked unhappily at her. Where was all that sympathetic understanding of a few moments ago?

He couldn't read beyond her enigmatic smile. Could she be trying to hide her real feelings from her father? Owen didn't know.

"Sit down," Tydings invited. "Tell me how it happened."

Owen sank into the chair next to him. He hadn't realized he had so many sore and tender spots until this moment. Again he sketched the evening's happening. "It was outright robbery of a helpless soldier," he finished. "I couldn't let that saloon owner get away with that, could I?"

"No," Tydings said softly.

Tydings had an alert, perceptive mind. Owen was glad to find it worked the same way his own mind worked. "I wouldn't be surprised to find that saloon is part of the Tucson Ring. Maybe you haven't heard of it."

"I've heard of it," Tydings said. "A loosely knit bunch of unscrupulous men with only one value in mind—to get as rich as they can by any method. Why does the Army let its people frequent such places?"

Owen made a wry face. "It takes some time to know which is which. Maybe this was the first time it happened in that place, or—" He paused a moment, then shrugged. "Maybe it hasn't been reported before. Men have queer streaks of pride. Maybe the others it happened to didn't want to report it." His voice sharpened. "It will be reported now. I'll talk to General Crook when I get back to Fort Bowie. Maybe he can't padlock that saloon, but he can certainly order it and a couple of others off limits to Army personnel."

Tydings stuffed his pipe, struck a match to it, and puffed until it was going well. "Isn't it odd," he mused. "Ask a hundred people here, and you might get one dissenting voice. The Apaches are responsible for everything bad that happens to Arizona."

"They have a big hand in it," Owen said dryly. This was the first time they had touched on this subject. That noncommittal observation was meant to draw Tydings out. Owen wanted to hear his viewpoint on the Indian situation.

Tydings stared straight ahead. "This may shock you, Owen, but the Apaches aren't always at fault. They fight brutally and savagely, but this is their land. They tried to throw off the invaders the only way they knew how, and I have a certain amount of sympathy for them. They were doomed from the start. It's an old story, constantly repeated in history: a stronger culture devouring a weaker one. The Apaches were up against a bigger foe, one better equipped and one who learned quickly. I look at them not as savages but as people who have families and homes. Their brutality is sickening, but it's a part of their culture."

Owen glanced at Stella. Her face was serene. Evidently her father's viewpoint didn't bother her.

Tydings shook his head. "I know this wouldn't make me popular in Tucson. And it shouldn't with an Army Officer." He puffed hard on his pipe. "What we're seeing here is nothing new. History teaches the same lesson over and over. There is no room for a weaker race." He looked at Owen, and his smile was twisted. "Maybe there's some reason for it; maybe that's for the betterment of mankind. But what we're doing to the Apaches is as cold-bloodedly brutal as anything the Apaches can think of." He was really wound up, for the puffs of smoke came faster. "Have you ever stopped to realize that the Caucasian race is the scourge of the earth? The Apache kills on an individual basis. The white race kills on a mass basis." He thought Owen was going to interrupt, and he gestured impatiently with his pipe. "I'm not deliberately trying to offend you. But I've thought about this ever since I arrived here. I'm watching what I've read so many times in history books. The white race does not go after the individual. No, they disdain to stoop to such a puny scale. They plan to wipe out whole cultures at once." He sank back into his chair with a sigh. "Owen, I apologize, but I was wound up."

Owen's chuckle made Tydings lift his head and peer at him. "Does what I said amuse you?"

"Not at all, sir. You should talk to General Crook. You'd be surprised how much you two sound alike. He considers the Apaches people, too. He got to know them well while he fought them, and I've heard him say in many ways there is no difference between the white man and the Apache. The Apaches know love, respect, and honor. This is the land they were born in, and the general thinks they should be allowed to make their home here. But the civilians are bucking him hard on that. The Tucson Ring has a lot of influence in Congress. The Ring wants every Apache moved to Florida. Congress is beginning to listen to them. I've heard our doctors speculate on how long the Apaches would last in that alien country. Florida has a wet heat, not the dry heat of Arizona. Out there are a hundred new diseases unknown to Apaches. Some of those doctors say maybe more than fifty percent of them will succumb to living in Florida."

"Will the Apaches submit to being moved?" Tydings asked.

"I doubt it," Owen said soberly. "As yet, they don't know about the proposed plan; at least, not that I know of. You've heard worried talk around town of a possible outbreak?"

At Tydings's nod, Owen went on in a harder tone. "I think you can count on it. Congress gives the Army the job of bringing the renegades back to their reservation. But they won't let the Army take over the issuing of supplies and maintaining order. The Indian Bureau appoints men who haven't the slightest knowledge of the Apaches and are less inclined to care. You wouldn't believe how the Apaches are cheated at every turn. The quality of their food is poor, the quantity short. No wonder they grow more sullen each day. They surrendered and agreed to go on the reservations because of promises made by white men." He glanced half-humorously at Tydings. "I never thought of myself as one of the destroying race, but maybe I am. I know this—if the Tucson Ring isn't barred from all affairs pertaining to the Apaches, we're going to have more trouble on our hands."

Stella had been listening quietly all this time. Owen said apologetically, "Stella, I'm sorry. I didn't mean to go on this long, but I got carried away, and—" He lifted his hands and let them fall.

She smiled at both of them. "I think it's a tie between you two. I knew my father was long-winded; his work trained him well for it." She shook her head. "But I thought you were one of the quiet ones."

Owen grinned. There was no censure in her gentle raillery. "I'm not trying to claim I'm a humanitarian. Lord knows I dread the thought of having to go out and round some of them up again. The Lord also knows the miles of mountain and desert I've ridden over to catch a handful of shadows."

Stella shuddered at the memory of past violence. "I've seen the wives of some of our wealthier merchants parade about town in their finery. Do they have any idea of the cost of that finery?"

"I don't know," Owen said somberly. "If they do, you don't hear any voices raised to stop it."

He started to say something more, then turned his head toward the front door. "I thought I heard a knock."

Stella jumped to her feet. "I did, too. Who could that be?"

A gloomy expression settled on Owen's face. He would bet that he knew. Captain Mundane was in town. Those cockfights hadn't lasted nearly long enough to suit Owen.

Stella went to the front door and came back with Mundane. He could lay that superficial charm on with a trowel. He was chatting animatedly as they came into the courtyard, and Stella was laughing.

The bubbling charm disappeared from Mundane's face the moment he saw Owen. His eyes narrowed, and his lips thinned.

"Hello, Neal," Owen drawled, making no effort to get to his feet. That enraged Mundane. He was a stickler for military courtesy, and he didn't think it should be overlooked at any time.

"Your duties must not be very pressing, Lieutenant, to let you spend all the time you want in Tucson." Mundane's tone was cold and remote.

Owen wanted to laugh. Mundane was unwise in choosing his words. He should be able to see Stella's face tightening at his remark.

"I sure wouldn't want to offend you, Captain," Owen said in the same drawling tone. "If you don't think I should be here, all you have to do is to say so."

That put Mundane in a bind. He glared at Owen, then glanced at Stella and Tydings. His thoughts were written in the congestion coloring his face. He wanted to order Owen out, but he didn't dare.

For the first time, he saw the swelling around Owen's mouth and the bloodstains on his shirt. "So you've been brawling," he said crisply. "May I inform you that an officer does not brawl?"

Tydings was angry, and it showed in his carefully controlled tone. "Captain, may I suggest you get your facts straight before you dive in?" He met Mundane's startled glance squarely. Mundane gave way first.

"Lieutenant Parnell went to the aid of a soldier who had been drugged and robbed in one of Tucson's saloons. I think that excuses him from what you call brawling."

Mundane was having trouble with his breathing. "What saloon was that?" he demanded.

Owen was glad he hadn't told Stella or Tydings the name of the saloon. "It doesn't matter now, Captain," he said carelessly. "It's all been taken care of."

How he enjoyed the alternating white and red that washed Mundane's face. He also enjoyed watching Mundane searching for something else to say.

"I'd better go find out about it," Mundane muttered. "I don't want the Army to get a worse name in Tucson than it has. My apologies, Stella, for making such a brief visit." He threw Owen a murderous glance before he turned to leave the courtyard.

"I'll go with you to the door," Stella said. The gaiety in her voice was gone.

"What was that all about?" Tydings asked after the two left.

Owen shook his head, his brow furrowed with thought. "I don't know," he said thoughtfully. "But it sounded like he knew where he was going."

"It did at that," Tydings replied. "But how would he know?" He paused before he added, "It would be interesting to find out."

Stella didn't linger with Mundane at the front door, for she was back in a few seconds' time. Twin spots of angry color glowed in her cheeks.

"What set him off like that?" she demanded.

"That's what Owen and I were talking about," Tydings said dryly.

Stella asked Owen a direct question. "You don't like him, do you?"

"No," he replied honestly.

She angrily tossed her head. "This is the first time I've ever seen him like this."

"Maybe it's the first time you've seen the real person," Tydings said. "I've told you before you always made your judgment on surface appearances."

Owen thought Stella would surely flare at her father for that. Instead, she sighed and murmured, "You could be right, Father."

# Chapter 5

Fort Bowie sat in a bowl surrounded by mountains, squarely athwart the infamous Apache Pass. That pass had known a constant bath of blood when the Apaches ruled Arizona. For several years, the pass had been virtually closed. A lone rider, or the driver of a wagon or coach, didn't dare use it. Even a stronger armed cavalry troop used the pass with the utmost apprehension. The presence of Fort Bowie loosened the Apaches' hold on the pass, and it was now open to all kinds of traffic. Even a lone rider rarely gave a second thought to the advisability of using it.

How well Owen remembered his first year at Bowie. Even a strongpoint such as Bowie didn't rest completely easy, for the surrounding mountains crawled with Apaches. Men could assure themselves that the Apaches wouldn't dare attack Fort Bowie, that the fort was too strong. The Apaches rarely attacked unless they had superior numbers and the element of surprise. Since Fort Bowie was favored by the terrain, the price of an attack against it was more than the Apache leaders wanted to pay. Nevertheless, these were the Apaches, and when all was said and done, they were unpredictable.

This uneasy peace didn't mean that life was comfortable and easy at Bowie. Life was still fraught with worry and strain. Every time a supply train was a few hours late, worry ran through the fort as men wondered if another train had been destroyed. That had been the case too many times. How often Owen had ridden out to the location of the train and been unable to do anything but sit and stare at the smoldering remnants of the wagons and the sad, mutilated corpses of men who had tried to take the train through. There was usually only one thing left for the Army to do: dig graves. The desert sands of Arizona were dotted with the graves of the luckless ones.

Now Owen sighed as he rode into the fort. He admitted things were better, much better, for the fighting had stopped, but at best, he could only call it an uneasy truce. One mistake, accidental or manufactured, and the fighting could start all over again.

A company of infantry was drilling on the parade grounds. It wasn't a new sight—the Army loved its drill and parades. Higher authority claimed the drilling was necessary; it made better soldiers and taught them instant obedience. Owen hadn't seen a minute while he'd been in Arizona that the drillings did anybody one damned bit of good. It certainly made for hot, tired soldiers, with a mouthful of oaths—thought, if not spoken.

The drilling company was lucky today, for the clouds hung low, almost touching the mountain tops. Maybe it would rain. Owen shook his head in resignation at the hope. He could remember similar conditions dozens of times, and he could count the times it had actually rained on the fingers of one hand.

As he rode into the stable area, Sergeant Reilly sprang forward to take his mount. He was a big, gruff man with a harsh, misshapen face marred with lumps and scars. Reilly was a tough sergeant. He enforced his orders with his fists, welcoming any rebellion against those orders. He had eighteen years of service behind him; two years more, and he would be eligible for retirement.

"Sir, the old man wants to see you. Pronto."

"Important, Reilly?"

A crooked grin moved Reilly's mouth. "Must be, Lieutenant. He's sent Atkins down here a half-dozen times to see if you had come in."

Owen beat the dust out of his uniform with his hat. "Then I'd better get up there." The imperative command to report to General Crook signified one of two things: trouble had broken out somewhere, or Owen had made a bad mistake. He hoped it was the former. That would be easier to handle. Owen had seen Crook's monumental wrath when somebody had stupidly erred.

"Good luck, Lieutenant," Reilly said softly. He took the reins and led the horse away.

As Owen walked toward the general's house, he checked over the past few days, minute by minute. He couldn't find anything that he should face with dread. All he could do was to wait until Crook made his jump.

The commanding officer's quarters was a handsome, two-storied building with a steep mansard roof and two sets of porches. Owen noticed absently that the south exposure was beginning to peel again, only a year after it had been painted. He thought with a grimace he sure wouldn't call it to Crook's attention—Crook hated disorder or disrepair of any kind, and had enough on his mind without Owen adding to its burden. Besides, whoever was responsible for keeping the house in repair was bound to catch hell when Crook noticed the peeling paint.

Corporal Atkins looked up as Owen entered. He blew out a soft breath of relief. "Am I glad to see you, Lieutenant." His face was round, and he peered nearsightedly through a pair of rimless glasses. If ever a man was unlikely to pick an Army career, this was one. But Crook considered him invaluable.

"He's been on my ass all morning." Atkins's tone held an injured note. "I'm not responsible for your whereabouts."

Owen grinned faintly. "No," he agreed. Some

of Crook's bad temper this morning must have spilled over on Atkins. "Where can I find the general?"

"On the south porch," Atkins answered sulkily.

Owen's face was sober as he turned away. Atkins's mood didn't augur too well for Owen: Crook had obviously been venting his wrath on somebody else until Owen arrived.

He stepped onto the porch. Though Crook didn't turn, Owen was sure he was well aware of his presence. Owen couldn't remember the last time he had seen Crook in a regulation uniform. Crook never wore the insignia of his rank. His usual garb was a weather-beaten canvas suit and a Japanese summer hat. Owen had listened to soldiers arguing over what to call the damned thing. Some claimed it was a pith helmet and not Japanese at all. None of them dared ask Crook to settle the argument.

Crook was of moderate stature, but as wiry and durable as the mule he rode. He claimed mules had more sense than any horse ever hoped to possess. Brigadier General George Crook was the only one who was able to contain the Apaches successfully. Former commanders had used the old tactics of the Civil War, tactics designed to fight an enemy that fought in large numbers and could be found in one spot. He had broken up the fixed, ponderous style of the Army, turning it into small, mobile units with speed the keynote. His coming to Arizona brought the mule into popularity, for all of the pack animals were mules. Crook had quickly learned that the best trackers of Apaches were other Apaches. He had built up the Apache Scouts, enlisting Apaches for periods of six months. Enlistment had its appeal, for he picked the scouts from the traditional enemies of whatever tribe was causing trouble. It was a clever move; Crook could always get all the trackers he needed.

Owen cleared his throat and shifted his weight. "General," he ventured.

Crook swung around in his chair, and those small fierce eyes blazed at Owen. His nose was prominent in a rawboned face, and his full beard was as stiff and bristly as a scrub brush. The Apaches called him Gray Fox because of the beard. He was an able man in many fields, and he had earned the troopers' respect. He could pack a mule, take care of repairing his own saddle, and was better than an average hand at throwing a rope. He also was a better than passable cook and never asked anything special for himself because of his rank. When he was aroused, he had complete command of every oath a professional mule-skinner used—working with mules enriched anybody's language.

"Did you enjoy yourself the other night, Lieutenant?" Crook growled.

Owen's eyebrows rose. He couldn't think of a

thing he'd done to warrant a scathing onslaught. But it was coming; he was certain of that.

"I don't know what you mean, sir," he said uneasily.

"I sent you to Fort Lowell to deliver dispatches," Crook barked. "That did not include a night of reveling in Tucson saloons. It did not even include riding into Tucson."

My God, Owen thought in dismay. The old man's got eyes and ears everywhere. But this time, whatever Crook's informant told him was wrong—at least, in part.

"I was not reveling, sir," he said firmly. "I did ride into Tucson. To see a friend," he finished lamely.

"A lady friend?" Crook said with wicked emphasis.

"Yes, sir." Owen didn't intend to budge. He couldn't see anything wrong in visiting Stella. "I spent a few hours at a lady's house. That does not constitute reveling."

Crook's face was growing red at Owen's repetition of his own term. "What would you call breaking up a saloon and mauling its attendants?" Crook snapped.

Owen took time with his answer. Should he, or should he not, tell Crook exactly what had happened?

"Did you break up Tribollet's saloon?" Crook asked impatiently.

Owen's head spun. How in the hell did Crook know that? Owen hadn't named the saloon to Stella or Tydings; not even to Mundane. Ah, he thought with sudden enlightenment. Mundane had to be the source of Crook's information. It couldn't have been Stella, or her father. But how had Mundane found out the right saloon?

"Maybe I should start at the beginning and cover everything," he said quietly.

"That could be the wisest course," Crook growled. His face wasn't quite so tough, and the blaze in his eyes was lessening.

Owen started with finding Mulvaney unconscious in the alley, of his suspicion that Mulvaney had been drugged, and of the doctor's confirmation. "He'd been robbed, sir. He said he had only one drink in Tribollet's, but his money was gone. I believed him. I've heard of other cases of the same thing happening to other soldiers. I didn't want this time to go by without doing something about it."

The gleam in Crook's eyes looked more friendly now. "So you did something about it?"

"Yes, sir. I found four soldiers who wanted to do something about it, too. I didn't even get their names. I think they came from Fort Lowell. It was quite a brawl, sir. Tribollet had two tough floormen. But I picked four good men."

"You let them do all of the fighting?"

"I couldn't do that, sir, could I? I took care of

Tribollet. I caught a blow in the mouth." Owen's hand rose. He stopped it before he touched his mouth. "Sir, may I make a suggestion?"

"Go ahead."

"I've heard Tribollet is one of the Tucson Ring. I'd like to see all of them smashed. It would hurt Tribollet in the pocket to be placed off limits to all Army personnel. At least, it would prevent another soldier being robbed."

Crook pulled at his beard, his eyes reflective. "An excellent suggestion, one that I've been considering for some time. You can consider it done. This isn't the first complaint I've had about that place."

The hollow in Owen's stomach was slowly filling. He wasn't going to get a reprimand for his actions.

"Aren't you curious where I got my information?" Crook asked.

"I am, sir."

"Captain Mundane came in earlier to file charges of conduct unbecoming officer against you. He said you did considerable damage."

Owen wanted to grin. "I guess we did, sir." He shrugged. "Some furniture was broken. One of the soldiers threw a chair through the backbar mirror."

The blaze was rekindling in Crook's eyes. Owen thought uneasily that perhaps his details had been too elaborate. "I don't understand how

Captain Mundane knew of all this. He didn't know in which saloon it happened."

"I think he did," Crook snapped. "I've had reports that Captain Mundane has considerable interest in Tribollet's." He beat a clenched fist on his thigh. "I haven't been able to confirm it. If I could . . ." He pursed his lips in angry reflection. "I'm well aware of the wide swath Mundane cuts. One of these days . . ." He shook his head and let the rest of it fade.

"You can forget the charges," he said in a quieter tone. "Captain Mundane hasn't been one of my favorites for quite a while. His rise in rank has been too meteoric." Crook scowled. "It only proves how valuable it is to have an influential father in Washington. I protested his last promotion, but Senator Mundane has close connections to General Sheridan. I have had complaints from General Sheridan about my handling of the Apaches."

Owen knew how rough that kind of interest from the commanding general of the Army could be. Sheridan would have easy access to the president's ear.

"But, sir, that's unfair," Owen started. At Crook's fierce glare, he cut it short. Crook could take care of himself.

"A man can't rise high enough to keep the wolves from nipping at his ass," Crook mused. "There's no doubt that Captain Mundane has written the senator about my rough treatment of him." His jaw had a belligerent jut. "Well, we'll see where all this leads."

Owen wanted to offer whatever help he could give to Crook, but he withheld his words: coming from a lieutenant that would sound ridiculous. He stood there, watching that keen, facile mind tear and pull at a problem. He knew one thing for sure—if Crook ever could prove that Mundane had an interest in Tribollet's saloon, God help Mundane.

Crook raised his head. "Lieutenant, you're close to Geronimo, aren't you?"

"I've tried," Owen said and let it go at that.

Crook nodded. "Captain Crawford is requesting you report to him at Fort Apache. He says Geronimo is getting restless. Maybe you can talk to him and find out what's troubling him." Crook used a minor part of his rich vocabulary in describing the situation. "An outbreak couldn't happen at a worse time."

"Yes, sir," Owen responded. He admired and respected Crawford. He had served off and on with Crawford's Apache Scouts and enjoyed the duty. It broke up the dull routine of an Army post.

"When do you want me to leave, sir?"

"Immediately. If you can find out what Geronimo wants, and if it's within reason, give it to him." Crook sighed. "I don't want that devil running around loose now. Keep me posted."

"Yes, sir," Owen said and saluted. He looked back from the doorway. Crook's shoulders were slumped, his head low. Owen wouldn't want the burden the old man carried.

# Chapter 6

Fort Apache was seventeen miles from the San Carlos Reservation. This was rough country, even for an Apache, and they were inured to heat. Owen had often wondered how Crawford kept his sanity in these surroundings.

Owen dismounted before the squat, tired-looking building that was the fort's headquarters. He tied his horse to the rack and walked inside. It was no cooler in here, but without the fierce sun cooking one's brains, the illusion of a relative coolness was welcome.

He entered a bare little office; an oaken table and two chairs were its only articles of furniture. A man worked at the table, his back turned toward Owen. His head was bent low over a stack of papers. He was stripped to the waist and sweating profusely. He laid his forearm on one of the papers. When he lifted his arm, the paper stuck to it.

Owen grinned at the burst of profanity. Captain Emmett Crawford was famous for his dislike of paperwork.

"Anybody around here know where I can find Captain Crawford?" Owen asked.

Crawford whipped his chair around, its legs scraping against the rough floor. He bounded to his feet and came toward Owen, his hand outstretched.

"Owen, I don't know of anybody I'd rather see right now."

"Then your choices must have run pretty low." Owen wrung the proffered hand. He frowned in mock bafflement. "How could I know it was you? You're out of uniform. Why don't you keep your bars pinned to your skin so that everybody can recognize you?"

"Horseshit," Crawford said inelegantly. "Don't tell me you'd salute me then. If you did, it would be the first time." A faint grin twitched his lip corners.

That was as close to merriment as Crawford ever came. Owen had never heard him laugh outright. He wondered if some tragedy marred Crawford's earlier life. If so, he had never heard him speak of it.

A strong bond of affection existed between these two, hammered out on the savage anvil of shared experiences against the Apaches.

Crawford returned the pressure of Owen's hand. He was an imposing figure, over six feet tall. His mustache and goatee were sprinkled with gray. His face was finely molded, cut by deep lines from nostrils to mouth corners. An indescribable sadness shadowed his eyes.

He was self-effacing in everything he did. Owen had never known him to claim credit for anything. He preferred to give the credit to somebody else. In the dog-eat-dog service of the military, it was astonishing he had risen as high as he had. Two things accounted for his success: he was thoroughly efficient, and the Apaches trusted him. They called him Tall Chief and Captain Coffee Cup—he seemed able to subsist entirely on that liquid.

"Sit down, Owen," Crawford said. "I can give you a drink of hot whisky, or a drink of even hotter water."

Owen declined both unattractive offers. He unbuttoned his shirt to the waist. "The old man thinks things are ready to blow. I hope to God he's wrong."

"Did you ever know him to be wrong?" Crawford grunted. He looked ready to explode. "I've seen some bad Indian Agents, but Tiffany is a new low. My God, it makes you want to puke. He came here with all the authority Washington could give him. That bastard won't listen to anything I say."

He's really keyed up, Owen thought. Things must be steadily getting worse.

Crawford glowered at him. "You remember his farming fiasco?"

Owen remembered. He had been here. But if Crawford wanted to talk about it, it was all right with him.

Crawford snorted. "Sending out harness that

was made for draft horses, harness much too large for the small Apache ponies. Even if the harness had fit, the ponies wouldn't stand still for those plows. They went crazy when a plow was hitched behind them, and ran away. Even if the plow didn't break up, its point was never in the ground. The Apaches thought it was the funniest thing they'd ever seen."

"I saw it, Emmett. It wasn't funny."

Crawford ran his hands across his eyes and suddenly looked very tired. "Hell yes, you were here. I keep getting things mixed up. Owen, do you suppose I'm losing my mind?"

"Like hell," Owen scoffed. He knew what was bothering Crawford. The captain had a sincere desire to do the best he could for his charges, but the pressure put on him by bumbling officials was crushing him.

"I think the Ring's got hold of Tiffany, Owen."

"That wouldn't be surprising," Owen said grimly.

"They're openly stealing the Apaches' rations now." Crawford's mouth was a bloodless, tight line. "Go into any nearby town and you can find Apache supplies being sold openly. A week's ration of flour isn't enough to last a day. I can't prove it, but I know cattle for the Apaches are held without water by the contractor until they're driven across the river just before they're weighed. The government is paying for a half barrel of Gila River water with each head. Rigging the scales to weigh heavier isn't enough for those crooks—most of those cattle are skin and bones; I don't see how they can stand. Hell yes, the Ring wants another Apache outbreak. Then they can scream to Washington for more protection. They want a few more regiments sent to Arizona. That would mean more fat contracts to supply more grain, hay, and provisions for the soldiers. This is the damnest nest of vipers I ever stepped in. I know, but can't prove, that the Ring is getting receipts for large amounts of supplies never furnished. Tiffany is getting his kickback for those receipts. I just heard that every Apache child upon birth is marked down for rations. Tiffany and the Ring don't let a dime go unnoticed."

Crawford ran down with a sigh. "I've really unloaded on you, haven't I?"

"You shouldn't give a damn what happens to the Apaches," Owen said. "Then it wouldn't hurt so much."

Crawford threw up his hands in a despairing gesture, then let them fall. "Does the old man know what's going on?"

Owen nodded. "He knows. He sent me down to talk to Geronimo. Is he ready to make a break?"

"Why shouldn't he be?" Crawford returned. "He listened to all the lies the whites fed him. Instead of promises fulfilled, he and his people are half-starved. Why shouldn't he be discontented? He can do better off the reservation. He won't have any trouble finding others to follow him; anything is better than what they have. If I walked in his moccasins, I'd be thinking along that line."

"You don't think it'll do any good to talk to him?"

"What are you going to tell him?" Crawford asked with brutal candor. "More promises we can't keep? Go ahead. Talk to him. You can't make it any worse."

Owen shook his head in sympathy. Crawford had battered his head so long against a stone wall that it was no wonder he thought his reason was slipping.

He smiled ruefully as he stood. "That makes everything encouraging, doesn't it, Emmett. I'll see you after I talk to him."

"I'll sit here and pray for miracles," Crawford said wearily. "My belly drops out from under me when I think of having to go after another bunch of renegades. That means more helpless victims. Everything we do works out to the Ring's advantage."

"It does," Owen said flatly.

At the door he looked back. Crawford stared at the far wall. His eyes were empty, but Owen knew his mind wasn't.

He walked outside and mounted. He had

another ride ahead of him. San Carlos was seventeen miles from here.

He was still thinking hard, when he rode onto the reservation. So far, he hadn't come up with the slightest idea of what to tell to Geronimo.

He passed the Agency buildings without stopping. The less he saw of Tiffany, the better off he would feel.

San Carlos Reservation was built on a gravelly flat at the junction of two rivers. Much of the year the two river beds were dry, or showed only a trickle of moisture. The cottonwoods along the banks were shriveled, their limp leaves hanging lifeless. The hot, searing winds were almost constant, trying to strip the reservation of all vegetation. The heat was a constant thing—one year of serving here was like being assigned to hell for an eternity.

Owen passed a group of Apaches. He knew several of them, and he lifted his hand in friendly greeting. Not one of them returned the gesture. Two of them spat in Owen's direction, three turned their faces away, and the remainder stared stolidly at him.

The chill of apprehension ran up and down Owen's spine. Conditions were worse here than Crook had anticipated.

Closing the Chiricahua Reservation and crowding all the Indians from it onto San Carlos was a serious mistake. But when hadn't there been a mistake in handling the Apache problem, he thought in dreary resignation. The Tucson Ring was said to have used its influence in Washington to get the reservation closed—maybe the Ring considered Chiricahua too pleasant for the Apaches. Owen grinned wryly. The Ring had screamed loud and piously to justify their move; they always did when they wanted to open a new avenue to profits.

Four thousand people were crowded onto San Carlos, land that originally held only eight hundred. Tribe after tribe was shoved up against each other without any consideration of ancient hatreds. Many of the bands were homesick. The mountain Apaches would never become accustomed to San Carlos. Tiffany seemed to be deliberately trying to make the Apaches' misery worse. He kept them on short rations, claiming for public consumption that keeping the Apaches hungry would force them to turn to the white man's way of life, making them self-supporting that much quicker. Owen snorted. He was still filled with rancor toward that idiotic plan. Farming was completely alien to the Apaches, and even cactus had grievous trouble growing here. They might have done fairly well as herdsmen and stock raisers, but farming? No.

Now they sat out their dull, monotonous days with nothing to fill their heads or hands and, too often, their bellies. Discontent festered in their minds until every thought was poisoned. This was a ripe opportunity for some enterprising warrior to recruit followers with promises of plenty of food, rich loot, and adventure. All they had to do was to leave the reservation.

That feeling of discontent had increased since the last time Owen was here. He could smell its noxious odor. Crook had asked a lot of him—to locate the instigator and prevent the rebellion. It could readily be Geronimo; his reputation had grown by leaps and bounds, and he had been behind other outbreaks.

Owen slowly picked his way among the wickiups. If Geronimo wasn't at his own wickiup, Owen didn't know where to find him. A half-dozen times he had stopped to ask information about Geronimo. Each time, the Apaches had stared blankly at him and hadn't answered.

If events had treated Geronimo more kindly, would he have turned out differently? Owen didn't know. Each man he knew, was pounded on the anvil of his own fate until he became malleable or turned brittle. When the latter happened, he was liable to splinter into a thousand pieces and fly in all directions, hurting whomever stood in his way.

Geronimo had become brittle, turning into the merciless killer men called him. He hated the Mexicans with a blazing passion, and he didn't feel much more kindly toward the Americans. Both had hunted him like an animal. Geronimo had originally been known as Goyakla, indicative of his earlier character, meaning "He who yawns." Geronimo must have been at peace with himself in his early life; he had married and fathered three children. His life was uneventful until the fateful day he had journeyed with the Bedonkohe Apaches into the Mexican state of Chihuahua on a trading expedition.

An Apache ventured into Sonora, Mexico, at the peril of his life, but Chihuahua was supposed to be safe. The trading had gone well. Each day, the Apache males traded and drank in Janos, a small trading town near the border with Sonora. But one day when the men returned to their camp, they found a scene of indescribable horror. Mexican irregular troops had attacked the camp, killing the few warriors left on guard and slaughtering the women and children, scalping them for the bounty the Mexican Government offered. Geronimo swore eternal vengeance, and for fifteen years he was the scourge of Sonora, his reputation as a successful war leader among the Apaches steadily mounting. He didn't confine his marauding to territory below the border, but extended his raids into Arizona Territory. When the United States tried to quell him, he amended his oath of vengeance to include anybody who tried to oppose him. United States troops were led on a long and bloody trail before Crook finally beat Geronimo. He listened to promises that Crook couldn't fulfill and surrendered.

Owen nodded to every Apache he passed. None of them returned the gesture, or acknowledged his presence in any way. It rubbed a man's nerves raw to see all those black eyes staring so steadily at him, far more eloquent than any words. Their friendship had been an uneasy one at best; now it appeared to be completely shattered.

Four Apache Scouts stopped him, and it was a relief to see faces that didn't stare sullenly at him. Owen knew Chatto well, the other three less so.

"Your faces say much trouble ahead," Owen said, stopping his horse and hooking one knee over the horn.

"Could be," Chatto granted. "Warm Springs and Chiricahua Apaches much close." He laced his fingers together and held them up. "It is said Geronimo is ready to be their war leader."

Owen nodded soberly. All he could expect was fragments of information from the Apache Scouts. Many of their people looked on them with scorn, and they were never admitted to the inner councils.

"Big tiswin drunk last night," Chatto went on. "Many warriors like this." Chatto waved his hand back and forth.

Chatto watched Owen with poorly hidden interest. What was Owen going to do about this? Drinking tiswin was a flagrant breach of Crook's orders. It was crude beer brewed by the Indians from partly fermented corn. Owen had heard some of the prominent Apaches argue that tiswin should be allowed, and they had a point, Owen conceded. The white man could drink his whisky. The Apaches resented that. Owen had tried to explain that the white man had better control of his whisky, where tiswin made too many Apaches crazy. He had never been able to change a single Apache mind.

"Bad thing," he said soberly. "Gray Fox will be very unhappy when he hears of it."

Chatto and the three Scouts looked uneasily at each other. None of them wanted to see Gray Fox unhappy.

"We thought you should know," Chatto said. His shrug dismissed the matter.

"Is Geronimo planning to leave the reservation?" Owen asked.

The directness of the question didn't make Chatto blink, but he did cast covert glances about him to make sure nobody was within earshot.

"Who knows what is in Geronimo's mind?" Chatto asked.

"Where can I find him?"

Chatto was only too willing to break this

contact with the lieutenant. He pointed to a wickiup a hundred and fifty yards away. "I saw him there not fifteen minutes ago."

Owen nodded his thanks and picked up the reins. He was grateful to Chatto for the meager information, but he wished he knew what was in that Apache's mind.

Three men squatted before the wickiup—Geronimo, Nachez, and Chihuahua. Owen knew them well from friendly and troubled times. This was one of the latter, for none of them returned his greeting, nor invited him to dismount.

Owen dismounted anyway. "You have nothing to say to an old friend?" he challenged.

Geronimo grunted, the other two were silent. "Friendship is an empty word," Geronimo said. He was short, as were most of the Apaches. His hair, parted in the middle, hung down to his shoulders. The high, coppery cheeks were split by two deep lines, running from his nose to a mouth so thin-lipped that it looked like an angry pencil slash. Two small black eyes, close to the bridge of his large nose, peered back at Owen. He wore the usual knee-high moccasins and a loose white shirt with a dirty handkerchief knotted at the neck.

"It doesn't have to be that way," Owen said easily. "If men's hearts are good, the troublesome things can be worked out."

He had spent many an hour talking to this

Apache leader. At first, he was surprised at the keenness of Geronimo's mind. Geronimo might be an unlettered savage, but he was no fool. Geronimo had once said, "I go the white man's way, for no other path is now left. The Apache must forget his way, or he will die. The white man is too strong, too powerful."

Owen stared steadily at Geronimo, wondering if he remembered. He was afraid Geronimo was deliberately pushing those conversations aside, for there was no warmth in his eyes.

Geronimo grunted. "Always words that have no meaning. One man can do what he pleases, the other must do as the first says."

"We used to be able to talk about those differences," Owen persisted.

Geronimo drew a deep breath, and his pent-up anger exploded. "Always white-eyes has his way, while he orders the Apache to do the opposite. Is this the fairness he brags so much about? We cannot drink tiswin, but the soldiers drink all the whisky they want."

Owen kept his wince from showing. Those fierce, sharp eyes had observed too many drunken soldiers. It was a fair indictment. This was no time to mention the big tiswin drunk of the night before.

Geronimo was getting heated up. "When I surrendered to Gray Fox, I did not agree I could no longer have the word in running my family.

Would you allow somebody to tell you how you must treat your wife?"

Owen allowed himself a faint smile. "I have no wife."

Geronimo made an impatient slash with his hand. "If you did have a wife, would you let an outsider tell you what to do with her?"

"In many matters, no," Owen said slowly. This had to be approached with tact. The Apache customs said that a husband could beat his wife—usually with a heavy stick. Crook had abolished that custom. "If I beat her so hard that she cannot walk, I would expect outsiders to step in and stop me."

"Paugh," Geronimo said and spat on the ground. "The white-eye custom. It does not hold for us."

"Does that include even biting off her nose, if she was unfaithful?" Owen asked softly.

"What would you do with her?" Geronimo challenged.

That was a ticklish question to answer. Owen didn't know. He hadn't yet been faced with such a problem.

"I would get rid of her," he finally said. "I wouldn't do more than that." Geronimo was bringing up all the old grievances, though Owen was sure these things weren't his real complaint. Those were old matters and had almost died out in recent years.

"You talk weak," Geronimo said scornfully.

"Such women should be punished." His English was passable, though often he lapsed into Apache. Owen knew enough of the native tongue to keep up with the conversation. The other two were following the talk, enough for both to nod at Geronimo's reasoning.

"But that isn't really what's troubling you," Owen said softly.

The blaze in Geronimo's eyes rekindled with new fury. "I am weary of being cheated, of being treated like a dog. All the promises given me have turned out to be lies. I am weary of seeing my people hungry and sick."

Ah, Owen thought. That's the real spur gouging Geronimo. "Gray Fox knows of all those things," he said quietly. "He is doing everything he can to change them."

Geronimo's voice rose to a shout. "How much longer are we expected to wait? Does the white-eye think another promise is enough to continue to hold us?"

Owen had that sickening feeling in his belly. Geronimo hadn't said so, but he might as well have put it into plain words. The Apache war leader intended to jump the reservation.

"Think long on it, Geronimo," Owen begged. "More bloodshed will not solve anything. It will only mean the return of the bad old days. But the end will be the same. The Apache will suffer more. Nothing will be gained."

"Am I to lie down and let you trample my pride?" Geronimo said hotly. "Maybe this time, the end will not be the same. We have learned much. Then, we were poorly armed. Now, we have revolvers and rifles as good as the soldiers carry. Maybe even better."

It took effort for Owen to keep his face impassive. What Geronimo said was true. Military commanders had been begging Congress for months, even years, to provide the Army better weapons, and Congress had turned a deaf ear. Owen had seen many of the Apaches carrying modern arms. Equally damaging, the Apaches had acquired experience at fighting the troops. They laid their ambushes more skillfully, and no longer fled wildly at the first shots. They could damn near be an even match for the troops. Too many officers would hotly dispute that, but Owen wouldn't deny the possibility.

The Apaches had learned to cope with the telegraph wires that once baffled them. It took time for them to figure out how the Army called for and received help so quickly. Linking the Army posts together with telegraph wires was probably the most important step the Army had taken in subduing the Apaches. In the past, when the Apaches jumped the reservation, they had ignored the wires overhead. Then, they had learned that to stop help from coming, all they had to do was to cut the wires. The Army quickly located those breaks and repaired them. Then the Apaches carried away long pieces of the wire, making repair more difficult. The last time the Apaches had tampered with the singing wires, they took away short sections of the wire, splicing the breaks with thin strips of rawhide. The splicing was done so cleverly that it took time and careful checking to discover the interference.

Owen drew aimless patterns in the dust with a twig. If only he could find the magic words to change Geronimo's thinking! From past experience, he knew how stubborn the Indian mind could be. Geronimo watched him with a foreboding expression. The other two exchanged covert grins. Geronimo had talked down a representative of the Army; he could do as he pleased.

"My heart is heavy for both of us," Owen said slowly. "If it was in my power to change things, you know I would."

Geronimo pursed his lips, then said grudgingly, "I think you would. We have not lied to each other."

"Let me talk to Gray Fox over the singing wires," Owen said. "Tomorrow, I will know better what will be best for both of us."

Geronimo wiped away Owen's words with a slash of his hand. "You would have me spend my life waiting for tomorrows that never come," he accused.

Owen stared at him steadily, holding back his denial. “Each man has to do what he believes is best,” he said. “Even though one man is wrong.” He straightened. This talk had drained so much out of him that it was effort to hold up his head. That familiar emptiness was in his belly. He hadn’t changed Geronimo’s mind in the slightest.

“Geronimo, I still wish you only good,” he said quietly. “I have always wanted that for your people.”

Geronimo would not look at him. “I believe you,” he grunted. “There are too few like you among the white-eyes.”

# Chapter 7

Owen's steps were dragging when he walked into Crawford's office. Crawford took one look at him, and his face turned gray. "The worst?" His voice was barely audible.

"He's going to jump," Owen said as he sank down into a chair. "Nothing I said could change his thinking. There was a big tiswin drunk last night."

Crawford beat on the table in impotent rage. He controlled himself and asked, "Would arresting the leaders do any good?"

"You'd have to arrest all of them, Emmett, if the tribes would let you take them. Have you got enough guardhouse space to lock up all of the Apaches on San Carlos?"

The grayness increased in Crawford's face. "Oh, God," he whispered. "There's no solution, Owen?"

"I can't see any."

Crawford briefly closed his eyes. When he opened them, they were haggard. Owen could guess the thoughts that were hammering in Crawford's mind: more burnings, more looting, more bloodshed. It would go on until the renegades were recaptured and returned to the reservation. It would be the same bitter experience, replayed at a fearful price.

"Maybe one thing would stop it," Owen mused. "If we could get double rations delivered soon—and it has to be soon—Geronimo might think it over. It could weaken some of the Apaches' eagerness to follow him."

"Where do you go to get those rations?" Crawford asked wearily. "To the Tucson Ring? Tell them it's to stop another break? My God, I can just see how they'll enjoy hearing about a break coming. The newspapers will fill their front pages, and Tucson will be screaming to Congress for more soldiers, more guns. Then the Ring can sit back, supply the new soldiers, and watch their profits flow in."

"I had a bad idea, Emmett," Owen admitted. He was bogged down in the same quicksand Crawford knew so well. Big trouble was coming, and they were helpless to do anything about it.

He stood up and said, "Guess we'd better get the news to the old man."

Crawford groaned as he joined Owen. "We're going to get a lot of people stirred up with just guesses. And that's all we've got."

"Should I go back and ask Geronimo for the precise date he plans to leave?" Owen asked sardonically.

He grinned bleakly at Crawford's black look.

Crawford left him with the telegraph operator. Owen wrote at length, then tore off the top sheet of the pad.

"For General Crook," he said.

Corporal Henley's eyebrows rose as he read the message. He threw Owen a startled look. "Jesus," he groaned. "Not again."

"I'm afraid so," Owen replied dryly. Henley was lucky. He wouldn't have to leave Fort Apache.

Owen restlessly paced the small, confining room. The heat was building up unbearably, with his emotions adding to the pressure. He listened to the rhythmic clacking of the key. The telegraph was fast, but Owen's impatience outstripped it. He was glad he wasn't at Fort Bowie; he could imagine Crook's outraged howl.

Henley finished and leaned back in his chair. He wiped the sweat off his forehead. "I hope you're wrong, sir."

"Both of us," Owen said fervently.

He couldn't stand long in one place, nor sit still while he waited for a response from Crook. The key finally started clacking again, and Henley scribbled as he listened. He finished and handed the sheet to Owen.

"Take what measures necessary to prevent outbreak," Owen read. "Sending one company from Fort Lowell and two more from Bowie. Signed, Crook."

Owen nodded to Henley and hurried out the door. He hoped those reinforcements from Bowie would reach here before Geronimo moved, but from bitter experience he knew the Army usually moved a step too short and too late. It was out of his hands now. Crawford would have to make the decisions.

His face lightened as he saw Crawford hurrying toward him.

"Raise the general?" Crawford asked.

Owen handed him the message. It didn't lessen the tightness in Crawford's face. "I've put the scouts on the alert," he said. "I'll issue them a thousand rounds of ammunition when we're ready to move."

Owen nodded. Ordinarily, no scout carried more than four or five cartridges, for they would gamble or trade them for what they wanted. Cartridges had a value of twenty-five cents each.

"So we wait," Crawford said grimly.

"Yes," Owen agreed in the same depressed tone. The waiting was what killed a man, but they could do nothing until Geronimo moved. He wished all the reinforcements were here; he wished Crawford had enough troops to ring San Carlos.

Friday and Saturday passed with nothing unusual, except the increasing pressure. Every passing hour brought a sigh of relief from Owen. With each uneventful hour he couldn't help but hope Geronimo had changed his mind.

Chatto shattered that illusion when he came to report late Sunday afternoon.

"Geronimo gone," he said flatly.

"Oh, goddamn it," Crawford exploded.

Owen had the same savage, helpless feeling, but Crawford expressed it adequately.

"How many went with him?" Owen snapped.

Chatto shrugged. "Not know. Some say many Chiricahua and Warm Springs Apaches go with him."

"See if you can find out how many." Crawford directed Chatto. "Owen, get a report off to the general."

Fifteen minutes passed before Owen returned. "Can't get through to Bowie. Wire's dead."

Crawford beat a fist into his palm. "The bastards have cut the wire again."

Owen nodded without speaking. Crook would be uninformed until the break in the wire was found.

"It's time to issue ammunition," Crawford said.

Owen went with him to help. The scouts lined up to accept the cartridges, laughing and joking all the while. They welcomed this; it broke the usual monotony of post life.

Chatto came back before the issue was completed. "Forty-two warriors go with Geronimo," he stated. "Maybe ninety women and children."

It was a frightening number to both Owen and Crawford. Some of those children would be boys, old enough and big enough to handle a rifle well. The long miles, the hardships, the bloodletting was big in their minds before they could hope to get those renegades back on San Carlos. Over four hundred Chiricahua and Warm Springs Apaches remained at San Carlos. The Tucson Ring would only emphasize the number that had gone with Geronimo. Arizona was in for another bloodbath.

# Chapter 8

The rising sun hit Owen full in the face, arousing him from his torpor. After riding all night, every muscle was beginning to scream its protest. He rode slack-shouldered and heavy-eyed, and his mount's step was dragging.

A fan of Apache Scouts was out ahead of the cavalry. They were excellent trackers, needing only a faint scuff in the sand, or a bruised leaf to keep them headed in the right direction. Owen was beginning to fear they had lost the trail during the night.

His fear was unjustified, for several of the scouts were beckoning Owen and Crawford forward.

"They've seen them," Crawford said, unconscious relief in his tone.

Owen knew the same relief. This could be one of those blessedly short campaigns, where the Apaches could be rounded up and returned to the reservation without the usual long, arduous days of pursuit. Owen didn't want to let his hopes rise too high, but from the actions of the scouts, it looked as though this action would be ended in a short time.

Twenty-five miles on the trail was about all the cavalry could stand. The heavy cavalry horses, carrying rider, the necessary forage, rations, and camp equipment, were spent and weary by the end of a day. Owen had known of Apache riders who could cover seventy miles a day. Each Apache had three to five ponies, trained like dogs to run along with him, so he could change from one pony to another before his mount was thoroughly worn out. He carried little but arms and ammunition, and it seemed as though an Apache and his ponies could subsist on nothing but cactus. Where the cavalry stumbled blindly in this vast, trackless land, the Apache knew every foot of it. He knew the location of every waterhole, and could go for forty-eight straight hours without stopping and still have enough endurance left to elude his pursuers. A week of steady trailing left the average soldier spent and dragging.

A half-dozen Apache Scouts stood on the edge of a sheer outcropping, looking out over a broad, flat valley.

Owen peered across the valley and saw nothing. The expanse could be as wide as fifteen or twenty miles, and he saw nothing stirring in that vast stretch.

He knuckled the moisture out of his straining eyes. "I don't see anything, Chatto."

The Apache had eyesight superior to a white man's. "There," Chatto grunted, and pointed. His tone carried condescension for the white man's weakness.

Owen followed the pointing finger and located what Chatto meant. Those weren't clouds at the far side of the valley; he should have known that, for the air was too clear. What he mistakenly took to be clouds were puffs of dust. They would hang there a long time in the lifeless air.

"Geronimo," he said flatly.

Chatto grunted, either in derision or agreement. "Dust made by horses he drives ahead of him." That could have been mockery in those black eyes. What was the white man going to do now?

Owen beckoned Crawford over. Crawford swore tonelessly. "Fifteen or twenty miles ahead," he said.

"Yes," Owen agreed. The hope of a short campaign was gone. He waited for Crawford's decision. Already, horses and men were weary. Owen hoped Crawford would stop, at least for a short rest. Geronimo's lead couldn't be wiped out in a few hours, or even several days.

Crawford made the same evaluation. "We stop for an hour's rest," he said. His eyes had that far-away, haunted look that Owen had seen before. Crawford knew what lay ahead of them. Before leaving San Carlos, he had taken time to pack sixty days' rations. Sixty days was a long stretch, but those rations might be insufficient. The pursuit could well take longer.

The scouts immediately stretched out on the sand. Most of them dropped off into an unworried sleep. The soldiers were too tired, too keyed up to follow suit at once. They sat with their heads drooping, grateful for the respite, but unable at the moment to take full advantage of it.

Crawford had ninety Apache Scouts with him, plus Troop A of the Sixth Cavalry. Second Lieutenant Grimes of Troop A was the only greenhorn. He was just recently out of the Point, and the fuzz on his lip didn't really demand a razor. He was bright-eyed and eager, and, Owen thought cynically, that will be beaten out of him. He could make this judgment through memory of his own first contact with the Apaches. There wouldn't be a great amount of fighting, only an occasional scrimmage that gained little. What Grimes thought would be the trail to glory would be only day after pitiless day of seemingly futile pursuit of shadows. The scouts would find those rare, scattered tracks that kept them on the trail. Crook had started the practice of keeping relentless pressure on the Apaches, to never let them rest undisturbed for too long. When man and animal wore out, Crook sent in new troops. It took a long time, it wore out men, animals, and material, but it was effective. If anybody had a better idea, it hadn't been voiced.

All around him, Owen heard the low murmur of voices. Some of the troopers cursed the situation. Those would be the same men who had cursed the dull hours of barrack life.

Owen moved over to Crawford and squatted down beside him.

"Never satisfied," he said with a grin, jerking his head toward the malcontents.

Lieutenant Grimes came over and joined them. He was a long, gangly youth. West Point had polished him, though he looked as though plow handles would still fit his hands. He was sandy-haired and fair, and the Arizona sun had already done horrible things to that complexion. His skin burned, then peeled, then started the same painful procedure all over again. Grimes was one of the unfortunate ones; his skin would never adapt to these searing rays.

Grimes shifted his weight from foot to foot. He wanted badly to say something; it was in his burning eyes.

"Something bothering you?" Crawford asked.

Grimes cleared his throat. "I was just thinking, if there's some way to cut them off, Captain, we could save ourselves a lot of time. Instead of trying to follow them, we could be waiting for them."

Crawford glanced at Owen, and his eyes twinkled. "Pretty good thinking, Grimes. It's too bad you're not on Crook's staff. He could use your advice."

Grimes missed the sarcasm, taking Crawford's words to be complimentary. That raw red face flushed with pleasure.

Crawford picked up a twig and drew a rough square in the sand. "Arizona. Follow me closely. I need your viewpoint." He drew two parallel lines on the east of his map. "The Mogollon and Black mountains. A favorite stamping ground for the Apaches. Should we turn that way?" He drew another range. "The Datils. They know it, too." He scratched out another line at the bottom of his map. "The Southern Pacific railroad. It should be watched. Nothing to stop the Apaches from crossing that, is there?" He drew yet another line. "The Patagonia Mountains running through south-central Arizona." His last line was a savage slash. "This is the border. What's to keep the Apaches from crossing it into Mexico? If they do, we only have to dig them out of the Sierra Madres." He made a series of dots along the border line. "Known waterholes. How many troops do we station at each one to keep the Apaches from using them? Then there's the Rio Grande to keep them from crossing. Oh yes, I forgot about the Burro Mountains and the Black Range. Which direction do we pick?"

Grimes sucked in a harsh breath, and his eyes grew round at the enormity of the job.

Crawford took pity on him. "That's what Crook has to think about. Miles and miles of practically trackless country, and all of it known to the Apaches. The Apache has one big advantage over us. He knows where he's going. All we can do is to follow him and hope he eventually wears down."

"I—I didn't think," Grimes stammered. He sought for other words and couldn't find them.

"No," Crawford said in sober judgment.

Grimes looked miserable. "I'd better go and look at my horse, Captain. I thought he was limping a little."

Owen watched him walk away. Probably wants to crawl, he thought.

"Too rough on him?" Crawford challenged.

Owen grinned. "There but for the grace of God and several years of experience go I."

Crawford chuckled. "And me. Give him time and he'll make a good officer."

"If he gets that time," Owen said soberly.

"Then it's up to us to see that he gets it." Crawford's tone had a bite.

Two days later, the scouts found evidence of the renegades' first camp. Hour after hour, they had been looking for some sign. Owen was beginning to fret that the scouts had missed something. Surely, Geronimo couldn't have gone this far without stopping.

Chatto and the other scouts prowled about a large area. Chatto finally raised his head. "Stayed here one night," he announced.

Crawford cast a startled glance at Owen. Geronimo had traveled a hundred and twenty miles from San Carlos without pausing to rest or eat.

Some of the signs he found puzzled Chatto, for he scowled at them. “Don’t know why,” he muttered. “Maybe big fight among them. But they split up.”

Owen kept his face impassive, though he wanted to rave. Instead of pursuing one bunch, they had several trails to follow. The forty-two warriors had divided. Chatto couldn’t tell how the squaws and children had split.

Crawford’s face showed the agony of his indecision. His command was the closest to Geronimo. If he made the wrong decision, he would expend time and energy uselessly.

He swallowed hard before he said, “Chatto, we follow the biggest bunch.”

Owen nodded approval. If he had been standing in Crawford’s boots, that would have been his decision.

“Mount up,” Crawford snapped. The rasp of his voice showed his increasing tension.

Owen looked at him with worried eyes. Crawford’s irascibility had steadily increased. Had too many miles of trying to run down the elusive Apache taken its toll? Was Crawford being driven near to a breaking point?

Owen swore softly at his fanciful thought. It didn’t take many days of this to draw a man fine.

Crawford kept up his maddeningly slow

pursuit for the next two days. The scouts were as thorough and skillful as anybody could be, but it took time to search for a tiny mark to determine that the Apaches were still ahead of them. Very few white-eyes would have been able to pick up those slight signs that Apaches had passed here. All the officers could do was to wait patiently until the scouts straightened and some of them swept their arms forward.

They passed two deserted ranches in those two days. It was amazing how news could travel. But somehow, it had reached even these remote spots. The Apaches were on the loose again. The deserted ranches were owned by wise men. At the first news, they had fled with their families and hired help to a safer place.

A thin plume of smoke halted the command at the end of a day. Owen waited while the scouts conferred with each other. No campfire, particularly one built by Apaches, would produce that much smoke.

"Been big fire up there," Chatto finally announced.

Owen and Crawford exchanged looks. This was what they had been dreading to see ever since they left San Carlos. This could be the first payment on a horrible price.

"Move on," Crawford said tonelessly. He didn't have to advise caution. Every man was well aware of the need for it.

# Chapter 9

What had once been a ranchhouse was now a charred ruin. This fire had been set yesterday, or even the day before, and only the smoldering coals trailed off little wisps of smoke. All of the outbuildings had also been burned, and they too trailed their small, individual plumes of smoke. Joined together, they raised quite a cloud, big enough to be noticeable for several miles.

Three mutilated corpses lay before the ruins of the house. Owen glanced once at the sad, obscene parodies of what had once been human forms, then kept his eyes steadfastly turned away. No matter how often he looked at a sight like this, it always jolted him like a mule kick in the belly.

He was glad that he had seen no female bodies. If there had been more defenders of this place, they had fled before the attack, or been carried away. Owen wished the three dead men had been wise enough to get out at the first rumor of impending trouble. But this was isolated country; it was entirely possible the three had been taken completely by surprise. He didn't expect to find any weapons. If there had been, Geronimo would have carried them away.

There wasn't a head of stock to be seen, except

for the four dead horses. They were big horses, bred for heavy work. The Apaches had slit their bellies; flies were everywhere, covering humans and animals.

"Mr. Grimes," Crawford said. "Pick out a detail and see that these people are buried."

Grimes's weak "Yes, sir" pulled Owen's attention to him. The usual florid look was gone from Grimes's complexion. He kept licking his lips, and there was a definite shade of green in his cheeks.

His first mutilated corpses, Owen thought. Owen wouldn't be at all surprised to see Grimes lose the contents of his stomach.

"Mr. Grimes!" Crawford's tone was sharper. "Didn't you hear me?"

"I—heard you," Grimes stammered.

"Then get moving," Crawford said in annoyance.

Crawford was tight-lipped when he joined Owen. "Don't tell me I was too rough on him," he said defensively.

Owen shook his head, and Crawford said angrily, "He'd better get used to it."

"He will," Owen said calmly. "But it's brutal when it first hits you. It comes too fast, not allowing you to pace yourself. Don't you remember the first time you looked at a mutilated corpse?"

Crawford looked suddenly old and tired. "That

was a long time ago, Owen. I guess I'd sorta forgotten how it hit me."

He glanced at the burying detail. Grimes was issuing orders. His voice sounded stronger. "When's the best period in a man's life, Owen? When you're younger, you don't know enough. Add age, and the increased knowledge sickens you."

"Tell me when you have the answer, Emmett."

Grimes came over to Owen after the burying was finished. That greenish cast was gone from his face, but his eyes had a murderous gleam.

"I made those poor, sad bodies a vow," he said savagely. "I promised that I'd avenge their deaths."

"Relax," Owen said. "You'll never get used to this, but it won't hit you so hard again. Don't be making vows you can't keep." This was Grimes's first contact with this side of the Apache. The other side had been a dirty, indolent Indian, seemingly harmless. The cost of knowledge always came high.

Owen's words couldn't satisfy Grimes. "They're nothing but murdering savages," he said fiercely. "That's all they understand. They wantonly killed those four horses and ripped open their bellies. They didn't even take the meat for food. I can understand hunger, but this other—" Grimes stopped and shuddered.

"They had a purpose," Owen said calmly. "The

horses were too big and slow, or they'd have taken them along. You don't see any other horses around here, do you? Those four horses had a use for the Apaches. They cut out the long intestine from each one."

Grimes frowned at him. "Don't tell me they'll eat that," he said in disgust.

"Those intestines will be as long as twenty feet," Owen went on, ignoring Grimes's outburst. "Knotted at each end, they'll carry a lot of water."

Grimes looked as though he was gagging. "They'd drink out of something like that?"

Owen uncapped his canteen and took a swallow. He spat to get the brackish, metallic taste out of his mouth. "I doubt it'd taste as bad as this water does. The Apaches wrap those water-filled intestines around their bodies. The water'll carry them over many a dry mile." He grinned mirthlessly at Grimes's distaste. "I've seen the time when I'd welcome one of those intestine canteens. You remember this: when your tongue's hanging out, the Apaches will be in good shape." His tone sharpened. "Don't treat them as animals with no ability to think. The Apache's natural cunning will carry him through spots where an educated man bogs down. Because he doesn't meet your standards, don't underrate him."

Owen shook his head as he left Grimes. He hadn't convinced Grimes of anything. Learning demanded a hard, brutal price, and it was slow in coming. Crawford had put it right; Grimes would develop, but he needed time. But first, he had to get rid of that hot-blooded idealism. That'll come, Owen thought grimly—if he stays alive.

The thin column wended its torturous way, always southward. Man and animals were jaded, and frayed tempers showed in talk and in animals' actions. Men snapped at each other, and an incautious man around the horses and mules could get his head kicked off. Owen had never seen rougher country. When the command climbed wearily to the top of one mountain, another one could be seen across the valley ahead of them. At times, Owen was positive that the trail was lost, particularly in the rocky stretches. The Apache Scouts cast back and forth, while the cavalry fretted and sweated. Then one of the scouts would find a dislodged rock, or a scuff in the sand. Then an arm sweeping forward would say that the trail was still there.

The monotonous days blended with each other until Owen lost all track of time. By the increased ferocity of the sun's rays he would guess it was at least June. He could find one small consolation: the pressure on the renegades hadn't lessened, though he hadn't seen a single hostile.

He rode beside Grimes. Grimes dozed in his saddle, his head drooping lower and lower, until he jerked it back up. This was a brutal lesson for a shavetail. The eagerness had faded from his manner, and where he had been voluble before, he rarely spoke now.

Owen was concerned about him. The seemingly futile days could drive a man to complete frustration. It cut away the thin outer sheath and disclosed the real inner core. Owen had seen other men break under such conditions. He didn't want it to happen to Grimes.

"We just crossed into Mexico," Owen said casually.

Grimes's head came up, and he looked wildly about him. He could see no difference in this country from the country they traveled over yesterday. There was the same hot sand, the monstrous shapes of the cactus, and always the blazing sun. Grimes's face was peeling again, and it looked raw. He had quit the painful task of trying to keep clean-shaven, and a sandy bristle covered his jaws.

"How can you be sure?" he asked sullenly.

"I know the country," Owen answered. "Don't look so startled. We're not trespassing. Each government has given permission for soldiers to cross back and forth over the border when they're chasing Apaches."

Grimes was appalled as he stared into the emptiness. "My God," he burst out. "Where does it end?"

Owen studied him keenly. Grimes could shatter, or harden into a competent officer. It depended upon how tough that inner core was.

"It ends when Geronimo plays out," Owen said. "Or when we do," he added. The latter could be the first to happen. He couldn't believe Geronimo was in as bad shape as the soldiers were. He was certain that Geronimo's horses were better off, for they had found evidence of three more raids on isolated ranches. Geronimo had obtained fresh horses, for tired, worn-out animals had been found at each place. Grimes had buried more bodies. The toll was beginning to mount.

Owen hated to look back along the line of the column. Ragamuffins rode scarecrows of horses. Men were wasting away under this relentless pressure, and the animals were gaunt. Rations were getting low, and this campaign couldn't go on much longer. Any day now, he expected Crawford to order the return to the post. If it hadn't been for a few head of wild cattle, the command would be suffering from hunger.

"Why does a man elect to go into the Army?" Grimes asked sullenly. "We haven't seen one damned Apache."

Owen's tone hardened. "Because he didn't expect it to be this bad. Did you hope it would only be parade grounds and fancy uniforms?" he asked scathingly. "This is what you hired on to do."

Grimes stared at his hands and wouldn't look at Owen.

No more pity for Grimes, no more consolation, Owen thought. Sure, this was a shock to him. But the transfer from the parade grounds of West Point to what Grimes was now enduring was too abrupt, too rough. Owen realized the wildness that must be flooding Grimes every time he looked at this ragged, dirty command. Grimes was trained to be an officer and a gentleman, but there wasn't a place for the latter in this arid country. There wasn't a whole uniform in the entire command, and bathing facilities were available only when crossing the rare river or stream. Owen was aware of his own rankness, for he could smell himself. He scowled at the long rip in the knee of his trousers. He had gotten that a couple of days ago when he had ridden too close to a thorn bush. White thread was all he could find to mend the rip, and it was a crude job of sewing. He was heavily bearded, and his hair stuck out through holes in his campaign hat. If it wasn't for the rawhide soles to his boots, he would be walking around in only the uppers. He was a disreputable specimen to be called a United States Army Officer, but he wasn't apologizing to anybody.

Owen searched for a remark to ease Grimes's torment. He said with grim humor, "Just when you think it can't get any worse, you can bet it will."

That didn't lighten the younger man's expression. Owen studied him. Maybe he and Crawford had made a sorry mistake in being too considerate of this greenhorn; maybe what Grimes needed most was several hard kicks in the ass.

He was pondering on how to start in on Grimes, when Crawford called to him.

Owen appraised Grimes a long moment before he spurred his jaded mount into a faster pace. Should he say anything to Crawford about Grimes's attitude? He decided against it. Crawford had too much on his mind to fret any longer over a boy who wore the insignia of a man.

He joined Crawford and Chatto.

"Maybe it's beginning to break up, Owen," Crawford said. "Maybe we're beginning to run Geronimo to the ground. Chatto thinks they may have located an Apache camp."

Chatto's eyes glistened. "Scouts report camp maybe mile ahead, maybe little more."

Owen wished Grimes could have heard this. Maybe it would brighten his mood.

Crawford squinted at the sinking sun. "We'll be in position to attack at dawn."

"Good," Owen said explosively. A dash of violence was what everybody in this command needed.

Crawford had the Apache camp surrounded before night. Men slipped into position with a minimum of noise, taking one slow, cautious step at a time. The camp lay before them, dotted by a dozen fires. In the flickering light of a dying campfire, Owen caught the shadowy outline of a horse tied to a tree.

It looked like a camp all right, but something rubbed Owen wrong. He had never known the Apaches to be so careless in locating their camps. The smell of this was all wrong. The fires had been built too large, with no attempt to conceal them.

The hour before dawn was the longest he had ever spent. The light finally strengthened, and shadows dissipated. Surely, if this was a camp, he should be able to see somebody stirring down there.

Crawford straightened and waved his arm forward. Owen heard a rifle shot, then another. He hoped somebody had seen an actual target and the shots weren't due to nervous fingers.

The command converged upon the camp from all sides, tightening the ring. With each step, Owen was convinced that this was only a decoy.

His conviction was confirmed when he passed the tired, worn-out horse tied to a tree. This camp was only a fake, set up to pull just such an action.

Men accepted it in accordance with their natures. Some swore dully, others stared blankly ahead.

"Goddamn it," Grimes screamed. "God*damn* it!" His voice rose higher and higher. The boredom and frustration had pushed him close to the breaking point.

"Shut up," Crawford snapped.

He took a step toward Grimes. Owen thought he was going to strike him. Owen touched Crawford's arm, and when Crawford looked around, he shook his head in warning. Crawford's face was set in a ferocious expression. Was this campaign beginning to get to him, too?

Crawford briefly closed his eyes. When he reopened them, the tightness was gone from his face. "I left a dozen men guarding the supplies, Lieutenant," he said crisply. "Get back with them and see that everything's all right."

Outwardly, Grimes's face didn't change, but Owen had the odd feeling that the inner structure was crumbling. Grimes turned and walked away without saying a word.

Chatto and a dozen of the scouts accepted the disappointment stoically. They trotted about the camp, inspecting the ground.

"Old stunt," Chatto reported when he returned. "Build fake camp, then gather someplace else. Found several trails where they left." His lip corners twitched, and he laughed. "Make big fools of us, huh?"

Owen couldn't help laughing. Chatto admired the skill of his own people.

Crawford looked at Owen disgustedly, then turned toward Chatto. "Maybe Geronimo is getting tired. At least, we're getting closer to him. We haven't seen this much sign in the last week." He pulled at his lower lip as he reflected. "We'll split up and follow as many of those trails as we can. Maybe one of them will lead to Geronimo."

Crawford gave Owen a half-dozen soldiers and a dozen scouts. "Don't get trapped," Crawford cautioned. "If you see anything suspicious, don't try to handle it with the men you have. Send a scout after me."

Owen nodded. He didn't like this splitting up. It could be foolhardy. Was Crawford getting so frantic that he was throwing ordinary caution aside?

Owen hadn't gone three hundred yards before he heard the thin, flat report of a rifle. That came from their main camp. He whirled and set off at a fast trot, tensed to hear another shot and dreading that it would come.

He saw six soldiers clustered over something on the ground. While Owen raced there, he heard two more shots, and he was afraid it signified a general attack on the pack animals. Owen blew out a breath of relief. Those six men were about a hundred yards from the pack animals. If it had been an attack, the soldiers wouldn't be gathered there.

He got almost to them before he saw what they were gathered around. That was a crumpled figure on the ground. A sinking sensation flooded him. He didn't have to get closer to recognize the figure.

Grimes lay face up. Owen stared soberly at him. Grimes had died quickly. His face was placid.

"What happened, Sergeant?" Owen whipped his head about at the sound of hoofs. Crawford had heard those shots, too.

Sergeant Harley's face was distressed. "He saw an Apache, sir. He grabbed up a rifle and ran toward him, yelling he was going to get one of those bastards. I couldn't stop him. I was afraid it was the beginning of a general attack. I had to protect the supplies."

Owen nodded wearily. "You did the right thing, Sergeant." Grimes had fallen for the old decoy trick. If the others had followed him, Apaches would have rushed the camp. Grimes had paid the ultimate price for his lack of experience.

Crawford joined them, and Owen explained what had happened. Crawford just stood and stared down at Grimes. Not a crack showed in that frozen facade of his face.

God, he can't be blaming himself, Owen thought. Crawford seemed incapable of moving. Somebody had to take hold of this situation.

"Sergeant, wrap a blanket around him and bury him," Owen said coldly. He looked again at Grimes before he turned away. Grimes had come a long way to find this lonely grave.

# Chapter 10

Another two days confirmed a growing suspicion: Geronimo was swinging north. It looked as though he intended to recross the border. Owen thought he knew the reason. Mexico was a poor land, with ranches and towns widely scattered. Geronimo didn't have access to supplies here that he had in the more prosperous Arizona. He needed food and fresh mounts. Owen could congratulate Crawford's command for one thing; dogged perseverance had finally worn Geronimo down. If he was going to keep running, he needed fresh supplies.

Crawford listened to Owen talk about his conjectures without replying. He hadn't spoken much since Grimes's death. His eyes were sunken in his head, and his hands were too restless.

Owen gave up trying to talk to him. Crawford was being gnawed on by several failures: Grimes's death and the inability to make contact with Geronimo. Crawford had no right to flog himself this roughly. He had accomplished one important thing: he had ridden into Mexico and turned Geronimo back. He had headed him toward country more frequently patrolled. When Geronimo recrossed the border, he was bound to run into one of those patrols.

Owen went to sleep that night, thinking about it. That's all he thought about anymore.

Crawford shook him out of a troubled sleep in the morning. "A sentry reports troops headed this way."

Owen's head cleared instantly. He sat up and reached for his boots. "Whose?" he asked.

"It could be our troops, though I haven't heard of any units operating down here. From where we are, I'd say it's Mexican Nacionales. The scouts are out there. They'll bring back information."

Owen didn't have time to get a cup of lukewarm coffee before he heard one of the scouts shouting something in his native tongue. The following silence had an unusual deadliness. Then the scout shouted again. The shout was answered by a fusillade of rifle shots.

Owen sucked in a harried breath. "My God, if those are Mexicans, they think we're the Apaches." He cursed savagely. "The damned fools should realize that was a scout talking. Geronimo would never give away his position like that."

The rate of firing increased, and bullets ricocheted off the rocks around the camp. Crawford had chosen his site well. Without the protection of the rocks, they would be taking casualties by now.

Apache Scouts began filtering back through the rocks, moving like flitting shadows. "Mexican soldiers," Chatto reported. He grinned bleakly.

"Waste much ammunition. They think they shoot at Apaches."

That sounded like Mexican irregulars, Owen thought. Those irregulars received no pay except the bounty they could get from the scalps of Apaches. They reacted overzealously, bounty looming large in their minds. Hearing an Apache voice was enough to activate their trigger fingers. Owen gave the regular Mexican Army credit for enough sense to investigate before they waded into a fight.

"Hold your fire," Crawford roared. He swung his head about to be sure that everybody around him understood his command. He glanced at Owen. "I've got to stop those damn fools before somebody gets hurt."

Crawford darted out from behind a cluster of boulders before Owen guessed his intention. He ran some fifty yards and climbed a prominent rock. He stood in plain view of the hostile force. His uniform was ragged and dirty, and Owen watched him with his breath clogging in his throat. Crawford was taking a hell of a chance in trying to get the firing stopped. Even those crazy fools should be able to see that Crawford wore an American officer's uniform.

Crawford pulled a handkerchief out of his pocket and frantically waved it. The handkerchief was soiled, but it couldn't be mistaken for anything but a flag of truce.

"Soldados Americanos," Crawford yelled. "Soldados—" He didn't finish. A volley of shots rang out, and Crawford crumpled. He fell on top of the rock, then slowly rolled to the ground.

Owen went wild with fury, and so did all of Crawford's command. Several offered to go out there and drag Crawford back, but Owen wouldn't allow it. From where he stood, Crawford appeared lifeless.

Owen raised a carbine to his shoulder and fired. "Just cut those bastards down," he choked out.

For an hour the battle raged. The scouts and cavalry used the shelter of the rocks to advantage, but with so many bullets being fired, it was inevitable that somebody would be hit.

Owen heard one man cry out, then another. After brief inspections he returned to his firing. Both soldiers sustained painful wounds, but they were not serious.

A hell of a lot of ammunition was expended with few tangible results. Owen ordered the men not to fire blindly; they were only to shoot when a target was in view.

He lay on the ground, the strengthening sun beginning to bead down on his shoulder blades. The sweat collected under his arms and slowly ran down his sides. He was surprised that the Mexican force would continue this long barrage unless they had far superior numbers. This was one of those senseless battles, started by stupidity and with no way in sight to end it.

He grunted as a white rag was raised on a long stick. The flag waved vigorously back and forth. It looked as though the Mexicans wanted to end this fight. The stupidity had run its course, or the American marksmanship was too hot for the Mexicans. Or there could be another reason: the way the Mexicans had been firing, they might be running low on ammunition.

Owen stood and waved a handkerchief in return. He saw a half-dozen men start out from the other side, and he selected five men to go with him. The two truce parties met in the middle of the field. The purported commander of the Mexican truce party was a lieutenant; at least, he wore a Mexican army officer's worn and faded blouse.

Owen looked at this apologetic little man. It was hard to keep his face from showing rage, hard not to curse him with every oath at his command.

"Señor, I am Lieutenant Cordova."

Owen made no attempt to correct Cordova. Maybe Owen's insignia was so worn and faded that Cordova couldn't see it.

Cordova looked as though he wanted to weep. "A deplorable mistake. I have many Tarahumaro Indians with me. I could not stop them." He raised his hands, pleading for understanding.

"But you could get them stopped now," Owen

said with icy contempt. “Did you suffer too many casualties, or were you running low on ammunition?”

Cordova flushed but managed to restrain this temper. “I have suffered casualties,” he admitted. “But I finally realized it was not Apaches I fought. It was Americanos. It was the Tarahumaros’ fault. They said Apaches were before us.” Again, Cordova spread his hands. “Señor, we fight the same enemy. I, too, hunt only the Apaches.”

Owen’s contempt mounted. He wanted to spit in this little man’s supplicatory face. “You jumped our scouts, Apaches wearing American uniforms.” That was partially true. Some of the scouts did wear discarded Army coats. Those Tarahumaros knew what they were. But here was great bounty, and the temptation to get it was too great. Besides, Crawford had stood in full view, yelling he had American soldiers. They couldn’t have mistaken him for an Apache.

“A full report of this will be made to your government,” Owen said coldly. “You’ll hear a lot more about this.”

Cordova’s face darkened with rage, and his eyes blazed. “May I point out to the Señor Captain that he is on my country’s land? I can arrest him, or shoot him down where he stands.”

“Cordova,” Owen said in open contempt, “you’re not that stupid. A dozen rifles are trained on you right now. One wrong move will be your last."

Cordova's cheeks tightened as he looked at the rifle muzzles protruding from between the rocks. He already had wounded and dead on his hands as a result of American marksmanship.

The conciliatory manner returned. "Why should we fight each other? We have the same cause—"

It was difficult for Owen to keep his temper bridled. He would have liked nothing better than to smash this oily little man.

"I'd advise you to move your force away from here as quickly as possible." The ice had returned to his voice. "If we see you again, I'll issue orders to open fire. Next time, it won't be stopped so easily."

Owen wheeled and marched back to where Crawford lay. Cordova wasn't worth another glance.

"My God," he said in disbelief as he looked at Crawford. "He's still alive."

Crawford breathed shallowly. The blood still trickled from the head wound.

He ordered Crawford to be picked up and carried back to the rocks. Crawford's eyes were closed. Owen didn't think they'd open again.

The meager medical attention that could be given Crawford wasn't enough to save him. Owen doubted that the finest medical attention in the world could do that. But it took two long days for Crawford to die. Not once did he regain consciousness. Owen would have wanted it that way for Emmett, if the choice had been his.

He watched Crawford's blanket-wrapped figure buried, his eyes cold and dry. The weeping was all inward. Rocks as large as men could carry were placed on Crawford's grave. Owen marked it well. The site was near the town of Nacori, Sonora; the United States government would want to recover Crawford's body and move it to a more fitting site.

Owen was in command now, and the responsibility was crushing. Rations and forage were very low, and it would be a struggle to even reach an Army base in Arizona. He looked at all those worn faces, seeing the anxious glint in their eyes. Every one of them knew their predicament.

It was hard to say the words that crowded up onto his tongue. To say them would be an admission of failure. He scanned those anxious faces and denied the failure. They had stretched sixty days' rations to more than double. They had kept inexorable pressure on Geronimo, digging him out of Mexico, and forcing him to turn back. No man could tell his part in this and know shame. Some other Army command would have to pick up Geronimo's trail.

"We go back," Owen announced. There was no cheering at his words, but men grinned as they looked at each other. He was sure they stood a little straighter.

He thought about Grimes and Crawford as he headed for the border. One had had too little time, the second too much.

# Chapter 11

Owen sprawled out in the chair before Colonel Lindell's desk.

"You look better than when you rode into Fort Lowell," Lindell said critically. He was a man of average height with a paunch becoming too noticeable for a good horse soldier to carry. That paunch had grown ever since an Apache bullet had broken a leg over two years ago. It had never healed right, and pained him constantly. He had gradually abandoned the field, turning more and more to administration. Owen knew how that galled him.

"How did you sleep?"

"I died," Owen replied. He only missed sleeping the clock around by a few hours.

Lindell nodded. "You looked like you'd already died in the saddle, when you rode in. My God, I never saw such a beaten bunch of men."

"They earned their rest," Owen said soberly. "I figure we rode over five hundred miles. God didn't make most of that country we covered. He wouldn't touch it."

He stood, and Lindell asked, "Where are you going?"

"To check on my men."

"Sit down," Lindell said brusquely. "That's all

done. I don't think any of your horses will be fit for service again. Some of the men won't be, either. Harley lost an arm. Gangrene."

"I was afraid of that," Owen said. He shook his head. "How about the scouts and mules?"

"Came through in good shape," Lindell replied. At Owen's grin, he asked, "Does that amuse you?"

Owen chuckled. "Just thinking of something Crook said. He claimed mules will outlast a horse three to one in this country. I know an Apache can outdo a white man." His face sobered. "Did Crook answer my wire?"

"Not yet, Owen. He's supposed to be in the field. He's going to take Crawford's death hard."

"I imagine he will," Owen said shortly. Crook and Crawford had seen a lot of service together. Lindell didn't mention Grimes, but then, he didn't know the lieutenant.

"Some of your scouts were willing to go back and bring Crawford in. I sent a mule train."

"Good," Owen replied. He was glad to hear that Crawford was being returned to his native soil. He didn't try to put his feelings into words.

Lindell was hungry to talk; it showed on his face. Owen had given him only the barest details before he stumbled off for a bath and a change from those rotten, stinking clothes. He had on his usual-size uniform, but it lacked a whole lot of fitting him now.

"I didn't have much to report to Crook, did I?" Owen said, his eyes moody. "Five months in the field, and I didn't see a renegade. Grimes was the only one who did, and it cost him his life. He was about three campaigns away from learning how to survive."

Lindell moved his lame leg and winced. "Some of them never get enough time."

Owen stared at Lindell. It was odd, but he and Crawford had spoken of the same thing.

"You haven't anything to hang your head over," Lindell said stoutly. "You kept Geronimo on the run. You wore him slick. There's a rumor going around he's ready to return to his reservation." At the brightening in Owen's face he said, "That's only a rumor. Nothing confirmed yet. A couple of squaws talked to a patrol. They said Geronimo wanted to surrender. I'm waiting for official word."

Owen shook his head. "I was hoping we could bring him in." He grimaced and shrugged. "I guess that will have to be done by somebody else. The Apaches really raised hell this time, didn't they?"

Lindell snorted. "That's putting it mildly. Geronimo ripped the lid off when he left the reservation. All of Arizona is gripped by terror, and justifiably so. You should read the newspapers. They're blaming the Army for total lack of efficiency." The colonel grinned sardonically. "You should have taken some of those writers with you. They'd have showed you how to do your job."

"Horseshit," Owen said sourly. He was more than weary of the men who sat behind desks and screamed how things should be done.

"This is the worst outbreak we ever had," Lindell said. "Two thousand soldiers and scouts combing these mountains and deserts."

Owen's sourness grew. "I hope they have better luck than I did."

Lindell's face was glum. "Not much more, Owen. You knew Geronimo's band split."

"That happened the first week he was out," Owen said slowly. "Crawford kept after the biggest bunch, hoping Geronimo was leading them. We thought by keeping him on the run, he wouldn't have time to do much damage. Were we wrong?"

"Some," Lindell said wryly. "Chihuahua's band attacked the Fourth Cavalry at Guadalupe Canyon. Killed five enlisted men and made off with horses and supplies. The Fourth tried to run him down. They managed to kill one squaw and capture fifteen women and children of his band."

"They have more to show for their efforts than I do," Owen said wearily.

Lindell shook his head in sympathy. "Chihuahua cut a wide swath through Arizona and New Mexico. He really smashed the outlying ranches. He needed horse replacements." Lindell broke a pencil between his fingers. "Left quite a few dead ranchers behind him."

"I can imagine," Owen growled. He had seen a little of that. Maybe they were lucky that Geronimo hadn't chosen a more populated area.

"Josanie, Chihuahua's younger brother, really made his elders look sick," Lindell went on. "In a month and a half it's estimated Josanie traveled twelve hundred miles, all north of the border. He killed thirty-eight people, stole two hundred and fifty mules. There's no guess on the value of the property he stole or destroyed. All that done with fourteen warriors."

"Looks like a young Geronimo is on the way up," Owen said bitterly.

"You can imagine how the civilian population of Arizona is screaming. The newspapers are demanding that Crook be relieved and every Apache be moved out of Arizona. The only way to stop what is going on is to get every savage out of the Territory."

"Those damned newspapers," Owen said in disgust. "Have they forgotten that Crook is the one who brought them peace before?"

"They say he's unable to do it now. Owen, I'm afraid this time that Congress may be listening to them."

Owen struck a fist against his thigh. "Let them keep yelling for Geronimo and the others to be moved, and Geronimo will never come in. I can understand that. This is their home."

Lindell smiled crookedly. "Don't try to tell that to the civilians. I think they'd lynch you."

"I'll remember that. I'm going into Tucson now."

Lindell looked startled. "Be careful, Owen. An Army uniform isn't too popular in Tucson right now."

Owen's face twisted in sudden wrath. "I wish to God that every soldier could be yanked out of Arizona right now," he said explosively. "I'd like to see all the screaming civilians handle the problem."

Lindell grinned. "That would be enjoyable. But you keep such sentiments locked up behind your teeth. You could start another war, and Crook wouldn't appreciate having to fight Tucson right now."

Owen's laugh was a short, wry burst of sound. "I'm just going in to see a friend. I won't be gone long."

"You'd better not. Crook could be screaming his head off for you."

Owen nodded. Despite what Crook said or did, he was going to see Stella.

He dismounted before the Tydings house. Those months he hadn't seen her seemed like an eternity. He wondered if she had changed.

Stella answered his knock. She stared big-eyed at him, seeming frozen for the moment.

"What's wrong, Stella?" he asked gravely. "Don't you recognize me?"

She squealed with pure delight and flung her arms about his neck.

Owen held her until she struggled to free herself, and he reluctantly released her.

She couldn't meet the steady probing of his eyes, and the blush on her cheeks deepened. "For a moment, I couldn't be sure it was you," she murmured.

He reached for her again, and she shook her head, denying him. "Father will want to see you," she said.

Tydings was in the courtyard, and Owen followed Stella to him. He wrung Tydings's hand and said, "It's good to see you, sir."

"And you," Tydings responded. He inspected Owen with a critical eye. "Your vacation didn't seem to do you much good," he commented.

"Father," Stella said indignantly. "Vacation! Of all things."

He smiled indulgently at her. "Didn't your captain say that?"

She flashed a quick look at Owen, then averted her eyes.

Owen stared straight ahead. So Mundane had been here. Owen wouldn't torture himself by trying to estimate how many times.

"Not exactly that," Stella said in confusion. "He said being out in the field should be welcome to anybody. It was better than the humdrum and monotony of daily life on a post. In the field, a man did about as he pleased."

Tydings's eyes twinkled as he looked at Owen. "Go ahead," he invited. "Say it."

"I wouldn't dare," Owen said gravely.

"Do you think I believed what Ned said?" Stella demanded angrily. "We argued over that."

The frozen look left Owen's eyes, and he could smile. He hoped that argument had degenerated into a quarrel.

Stella was still upset with her father, for she said heatedly, "Don't you think I could look at Owen and see what he's gone through? He's so thin."

She looked at Owen as she spoke. Tydings winked at Owen. Tydings was on Owen's side all the way.

"Tell us about it," Tydings invited. "All we get are the newspaper's report. I'm afraid they're distorted."

Owen wouldn't commit himself. "They could be," he admitted.

He was silent, and Tydings prodded him. "We're getting reports that Geronimo may surrender."

"I hope so," Owen said fervently. "Though I haven't heard a thing about it. We chased him a long way without catching a glimpse of him. If he's half as weary of running as I am, then I'd say he's more than ready to come in."

"It was awful, wasn't it?" Stella burst out.

Owen reflected a moment before he answered. He thought of Grimes's and Crawford's deaths. Awful could readily be a mild word.

"There were some things I didn't like," he said with a rueful grin. "The food wasn't very good." He remembered vividly living on parched corn for two solid weeks. The taste of it was still in his mouth. Finding that small patch of stunted corn in Mexico had enabled them to go on. But he didn't think he ever wanted to eat corn again.

"Our uniforms wore out. The sweat rotted them, and they ripped easily." He glanced with humor at Stella. "You couldn't have the slightest idea of how bad a human body can smell when it goes day after day without washing."

His word-picture must have been vivid, for she crinkled up her nose. She shuddered and murmured, "I'm glad I wasn't born a man."

Owen smiled. "I'm kinda glad you weren't, too."

She made a face at him and jumped to her feet. "I baked a cake today. Could I tempt you?"

He closed his eyes in rapture. "Try me and see."

Tydings waited until Stella left the courtyard. "You're giving her the lighter, funny side of it," he accused.

"Yes," Owen admitted. "It's the small irritations and discomforts that stick in a man's mind. The body lice bothered me most." He grinned at Tydings's expression. "You haven't known them? Maybe I can get you a stretch in the Army."

"No, thanks," Tydings said hastily. "Did the lice really get that bad?"

"Without any exaggeration," Owen said solemnly. "I'd ride along, trying not to think of them, and the itching drove me crazy."

Tydings's interest showed. "Couldn't you get rid of them?"

"We could, if we were lucky enough to find two things together. Shade and an anthill."

Owen smiled at the puzzled look on Tydings's face. "We had to strip down. That sun blisters a bare body. After a stick stirred up that anthill, you spread your clothes on the hill and waited. The big red ants were the best. I don't know whether they were mad or hungry, but they sure took care of the cooties. That gave us relief for a while."

Tydings grimaced. "I'm like Stella. I'm glad I wasn't born to be a soldier."

Owen nodded. "Particularly in Arizona."

"Why do you stay in the Army, Owen?"

"I've asked myself that question dozens of times." Owen allowed himself to think briefly of Emmett Crawford. Crawford must have asked himself the same question. He had died without the answer.

Owen shook his head. "I don't know. It pays poorly, and if it leads to glory, it's a slow trail." He shook his head again. "I guess somebody's got to do it," he finished quietly.

Before Tydings answered, Stella returned with a plate of cake and a pitcher of milk. "The milk isn't cold," she apologized.

Owen thought of the gallons of brackish, metallic-tasting water he had drunk. Anything after that would be welcome.

He took a bite of his cake, his eyes sparkling with approval. "I'm learning how many accomplishments you have."

Stella's cheeks tinged with color at the compliment. She laughed and said, "You're just comparing it to that parched corn."

Owen smiled. The smile changed to a frown at the knock on the door.

Stella spoke the question in Owen's mind. She also frowned. "Now who could that be?"

Owen was heavy-faced. He thought he could guess.

Stella answered the knock and returned with Captain Neal Mundane behind her. He was bubbling with his usual charm. Stella hadn't said anything about Owen being there, for the bubbling was choked off, and Mundane's face darkened as he saw Owen.

He tried to regain his light, airy spirits and found it difficult going. "So you finally decided to come back to work." The words had a nasty undertone.

"I decided to try your way," Owen said softly. "I found out that riding a desk is easier than a saddle."

Mundane's lips thinned, and his breathing quickened. Owen noticed with satisfaction that Mundane was putting on weight. His stomach was bulging over his belt. Mundane's eyes were wicked as he said, "You're way off the trail, if you think my job is easy."

Owen's eyes danced. He had successfully goaded Mundane. If he could keep it up, he might force Mundane into unwise remarks.

"Not at all," he disclaimed. "Sitting under the shade of a hot roof must be wearing on a man. And the monotony of regular meals and good food . . ." He shook his head. "That has to be wearing on a man's nerves. Going into town whenever you please couldn't begin to break up the monotony."

Mundane's cheeks were purpling. "By God," he said hotly, "I'd like to have you under my command for a while. If you think ordering supplies and keeping them distributed is a cinch, I'd teach you different in a hurry."

"Tough job," Owen murmured. "All kinds of hitches—irresponsible agents and the like. Never able to get it all through. Crawford sure didn't get his share."

That remark shoved Mundane over the edge. He forgot that Stella and Tydings were present. "Why, goddamn it," he sneered. "If you're trying to lay blame, take some for yourself. You sure as hell didn't accomplish anything."

Tydings frowned, and Stella's face went rigid with anger. "That's enough, Neal," she said sharply. "That's pretty unfair."

Mundane glared at her. His rage reached out and included her. "If I'm intruding . . ." he sneered. Mundane didn't know her at all. He missed those sparks in her eyes.

"You might be doing just that," she said stiffly.

"I can find the front door," Mundane said. His tone had weakened. He hoped Stella would beg him to stay.

"I'm sure you can," she agreed.

Mundane's blazing eyes raked Owen. "You haven't heard the last of this," he said thickly. He wheeled and strode toward the front door.

Owen heard the savage thrusts of his heels all the way there. Mundane used unnecessary force slamming the door behind him.

"I'm sorry, Stella," Owen apologized. He was lying; he wasn't sorry at all.

"For what?" she said angrily. "Did you think you had to take whatever he wanted to say without replying?" Anxiety crept into her tone. "Can he make it difficult for you?"

Owen wanted to laugh with the elation swelling

within him. He shook his head. "I don't work for him. I'm not a desk officer." Something had happened to change Stella's view of Mundane. It might have happened abruptly tonight, or it could have been a gradual thing over the past months. He glanced at Tydings. Tydings was trying to hide a covert smile.

"Something's happened to change him," Stella said thoughtfully.

Tydings tried to hide his snort and wasn't successful.

"Well, it has," Stella said defensively. "He's not the same at all."

Owen was wise enough to know when to change the subject. He took another bite of his cake. "Best cake I ever ate," he said happily.

# Chapter 12

Captain Neal Mundane was furious as he strode down Main Street. He was vaguely aware of hostile glances thrown his way, and he heard a few oaths directed at "the worthless goddamned Army." Those glances and oaths were from the common men, and Mundane didn't give a damn what the stupid oafs thought. He knew what the higher class of men, the rich, intelligent ones, thought. They treated him with respect and welcomed his company.

That goddamned Parnell, he raged as he strode along. He wished there was some way to smash him. He had tried that once after Tribollet's saloon had been wrecked. He still shuddered as he thought of Crook's calling him down over that. Mundane had concluded wisely that he'd better keep his hands and tongue off Lieutenant Parnell.

He noticed few military men on the streets tonight. Most of them were in the field after the Apaches. It cut his income one way, but it increased it another. An interest in Tribollet's saloon wasn't nearly as important as a percentage of Travis Ulman's lucrative hay and grain contracts with the Army.

His lips curled wrathfully as he thought of Stella. She'd made her preference plain tonight.

She would regret that when he wound up a wealthy man. Mundane had considered her to be a highly intelligent woman. She wasn't when she backed a lieutenant. She would learn in a hurry just how little a lieutenant's pay was.

He walked into Ulman's office, and Travis Ulman nodded, acknowledging his presence. As usual, Ulman looked harassed by the rush of his business. His desk was littered with papers. He discussed some of them with clerks and scrawled his name on others.

Mundane settled down across from Ulman. He enjoyed seeing Ulman being rushed like this. He got a small percentage out of every dollar Ulman made.

"I hope Geronimo stays out forever," he said and grinned.

Ulman observed Mundane thoughtfully. "I don't want to be disturbed for a while," he said, dismissing the clerks.

He waited until they were gone before he spoke. "I'm afraid you're not going to get your wish."

Mundane frowned. "What do you mean?"

Ulman made an impatient gesture. "Haven't you heard the rumor? Geronimo may be getting tired of running."

Mundane leaned back, and his grin returned. "Just talk. You know how talk is."

"I'm afraid this one has basis," Ulman said

regretfully. “A buck and two squaws from Geronimo’s bunch came in to Fort Apache. Geronimo wants to talk to General Crook.” He pointed a meaningful finger at Mundane. “Geronimo surrendered to Crook before. It looks as though it’s habit-forming.”

He smiled grimly at the dismay that flooded Mundane’s features. “There’s even talk that the meeting place has been set. It’s supposed to be at Cañon de los Embudos. Geronimo’s a sly one. He picked a point a few miles south of the border. If something goes wrong, he can duck deeper into Mexico.”

Mundane sat there aghast. If Geronimo actually surrendered, it meant the return of an uneasy peace. All the need for the fat contracts from the Army would be gone. He could kiss his percentage in them good-bye.

“You’d better get word to the senator,” Ulman said. “If Crook could be removed, perhaps Geronimo wouldn’t talk to another general.”

Mundane nodded numbly, his mind digging at the debris left by the shattering of his dreams. His father didn’t like Crook; Senator Mundane would gladly do everything possible to see him removed from command. But was there enough time for any action to be taken, before Crook’s meeting with Geronimo?

His mind skipped about, trying to find a solid purchase. His eyes gleamed as he thought of something. “Is there still talk of moving the Apaches to Florida?”

“Stronger than ever,” Ulman replied. “This time, I think Congress will act on it. Even the eastern newspapers are putting pressure on Congress.” He bared his teeth in a mirthless grin. “Personally, I’d hate to see it happen. The Apaches are good for business.”

“Would Geronimo surrender if he got word of that move?”

Ulman pulled at his lower lip. “I doubt he would. But how’s he going to hear about it?”

Mundane stood, his eyes excited. “Maybe there’s a way. I’ll let you know if it works out.”

He looked back from the door. Ulman’s head was bent again over his paperwork. Ulman wasn’t much of a dreamer. He would take care of the business that was on hand.

Mundane entered Tribollet’s saloon by the rear door. Tribollet was just coming out of his office. He looked at Mundane and stepped back inside. Mundane had something on his mind.

Tribollet poured the good whisky he kept for his personal use, and Mundane gulped down his drink.

“How’s business?” Mundane asked.

“You know that, boss. Your share ain’t been so hot. People meet outside and talk about the Apaches. They don’t come in and drink like they used to. We ain't hardly getting any soldier trade at all."

Mundane wasn't doing too well here, but he was more than making it up with Ulman. The balance more than leaned in his favor.

"Have you heard talk of Geronimo surrendering?"

"Hell, nothing but talk ever since he broke out. None of it means anything."

"Maybe this time it does. The surrender talk has gone so far there's talk of him and Crook meeting at Cañon de los Embudos. Do you know where that is?"

"Just across the border. I've been there," Tribollet said indifferently.

Mundane eyed him shrewdly. "Could you get to Geronimo without the Army knowing anything about it?"

Tribollet scowled as he reflected upon that. "I've sold the old bastard a lot of whisky. I could get to him, if he's really quitting the warpath. Him and the Army won't camp together, I don't care how much they talk. Geronimo is one suspicious Apache. Unless he gets the terms he wants, he won't go to sleep with the Army anywhere around him."

Mundane's breathing came faster. This was going better than he had hoped. "Would two hundred dollars make it worth your while to try and talk to him?"

Tribollet's eyes glistened. "For that much, I'd go into hell and talk to the devil. I'll take some whisky with me. Geronimo ought to be really dry by now. He'll listen. What do you want me to say to him?"

"Tell him the Army plans to murder him the minute he crosses the border. What Apaches are left, the Army will ship to Florida. Either way, he'll never see Arizona again."

Tribollet looked at him appraisingly. "You know what that means?"

"You tell me," Mundane said and grinned.

"That'd make him cut out again."

Mundane's grin grew broader. "It sure would, wouldn't it? Hell, I never thought of that."

# Chapter 13

Owen rode with General Crook at the head of the long column wending its way toward Cañon de los Embudos. A peace parley supposedly lay ahead of them, but Crook never relaxed his precautions. The Apache Scouts were out ahead of the column, checking every yard of the way to attest to its safety.

It had been a long ride from Fort Bowie, passing White's ranch and Mud Springs, but the urgency of Owen's earlier ride no longer existed. A few more hours no longer mattered; before, it could have meant losing contact with the renegades. The column watered at Contrabandista Springs, then rode down the dry bed of the Rio de San Bernardino, turning east into the canyon, opposite the Sierra de los Embudos.

The column was in good spirits, and troopers sang at the evening camps. Everybody seemed lighthearted except Crook. A heavy mood had held him ever since Fort Bowie fell behind them. Crook brooded in silence, and if somebody dared break that silence, he snapped at them.

Owen wondered why. He would have thought Crook would be optimistic. If the surrender talk went well, Crook had again ended the terror in Arizona.

"It'll work this time, sir," Owen ventured.

Crook cast him an odd glance. "Will it?" he asked waspishly. "It better. Washington's been on my back too long."

By Washington, Owen was sure Crook meant General Sheridan. An Army career was a vicious ladder. No matter how hard a man struggled to climb another rung, there was always somebody ahead of him.

"I want you with me when I talk to Geronimo," Crook said. "You seem to have as much influence on him as anybody."

Owen laughed ruefully. "I didn't do so well with him the last time." To be honest, after Fort Apache, he hadn't even seen Geronimo.

"Who did?" Crook said shortly.

The ravine was a beautiful place, and Owen compared it with some of the land he had covered in the past months. It was too bad Crawford's campaigning hadn't been conducted in Cañon de los Embudos. Water ran down the middle of the canyon, and its musical flow murmured peace in a man's ears. Tall, slender sycamores, ash, cottonwoods, and willows shadowed the canyon's length. In places the thorny buckthorn and other vegetation grew so thickly a horse could barely force a passage. Water was the reason for that growth. All of this land would be fruitful, if only water was present.

"The scouts are leading Geronimo in, sir."

Owen pointed out the group of horsemen approaching from the other end of the canyon.

Crook nodded without speaking. He had seen them.

The squaws and small children plodded behind the warriors. It looked as though all the prominent Apache leaders of the renegades were here. Owen recognized Geronimo, Nachez, Chihuahua, Nana, and Josanie.

"It looks as though they mean business this time," Owen said.

Crook's piercing eyes rested on him. "I hope to God you're right, Lieutenant."

His voice was oddly heavy. Owen felt a shiver run down his spine. Crook had an instinct that was rarely wrong. Did some premonition warn him that this wasn't over yet? If so, Owen fervently hoped that premonition was wrong.

Owen made a rapid count of the warriors as the two forces converged. Some of the bucks were missing. That could be due to attrition, battles costing Geronimo dead and wounded. Boys, armed with rifles and cartridge belts, would make up for some of the missing warriors.

Geronimo didn't seem to be in dire straits. Every fighting man wore two cartridge belts, and light reflected from the metallic bases of the cartridges stuffed into the loops. Starvation hadn't marked any of them, and Owen didn't see a worn-out pony. Every male wore a brand-new shirt, the kind made of German cotton in Mexico. Most of the males wore new parti-colored blankets. Geronimo had bought them, or plundered them in Mexico.

The greeting between the two forces was brief. Owen thought he detected a listlessness in the Apaches' manner, and a haggardness in their faces. Their new clothes might be making a brave display, but they couldn't hide the bone-deep weariness they felt.

"It is more comfortable to talk sitting on the ground," Geronimo said and dismounted. All of the other warriors followed suit. Not a one of them released his rifle.

Crook swung down from his mule and picked a spot in heavy shade. Geronimo settled down, facing him.

"I have come a long way," Crook said testily. "What have you to say?"

Geronimo recounted a lengthy list of real or fancied abuses. "Not once have I lied to you, nor have you lied to me. But other men have lied to me many times."

"Two years ago when you surrendered to me, you lied," Crook said bluntly. "You promised to live in peace. When a man lies to me, it is hard to trust him again."

Geronimo looked agitated. Even though he sat in the shade, he sweated profusely. He pulled and twisted at a rawhide thong he held.

"I am not a bad man," he protested. "Though I know many say I am. The Indian Agents are the bad men. If they treat us as they should, then I am willing to live in peace."

The talk went on for hours. Progress was necessarily slow, for everything had to be translated. Geronimo made no attempt to say anything in English. He let the two official interpreters handle the translation. Owen wouldn't trust his Apache that much to enter into the conversation. He tried to judge how the talk was going by the expressions on Crook's and Geronimo's faces. He couldn't tell much. That heavy frown never left Crook's face. Geronimo alternately cajoled, begged, and stormed.

"I can leave again," he threatened.

Crook nodded. "You can. You must make up your own mind to one of two things. You can stay out on the warpath, or surrender unconditionally. If you do not return, I'll keep after you and kill every warrior. Even if it takes me fifty years."

Fierce white eyes stared at fierce Indian eyes. Geronimo looked away first.

Crook's statement startled Owen. Crook wouldn't live the fifty years of his threat. But it might take the Army that much time trying to dig Geronimo out of Sonora, Mexico.

Geronimo sighed mournfully. "I am getting old and tired. I want only to live in peace. You promise me that all of us can return to San Carlos?"

“There will be some punishment,” Crook stated flatly. “The leaders must be sent east and imprisoned there. You can take your families with you. After that, you can return to Arizona. I will do everything to see that honorable men are appointed as agents.”

Geronimo stared at the ground for a long time. Owen listened to the murmur of warriors’ voices as they digested the interpreter’s words. By the sound of the voices, they were bitter words to swallow.

“How much time do we have to stay in the east?” Geronimo finally asked.

“Two years. No more.” Some of the fierceness was leaving Crook’s face.

“Two years isn’t the longest time in a man’s life,” Geronimo said. “I will talk it over tonight and see you in the morning.”

“Agreed,” Crook said abruptly. He stood and stalked away.

Owen followed and found Crook seated before his tent. “Will they be back?” Owen asked.

“I think so. I hope so,” Crook said heavily. “I promised them more than I was authorized to.” He stared into the distance. “I never broke a promise to them. I’d hate to start now.”

“Yes,” Owen said simply.

The Apache chieftains sat in conference far into the night. Some argued fiercely against what

Crook offered, others were in favor of accepting.

"My heart is tired of running," Geronimo said slowly. "If we keep on, what is ahead of us? Only death. You heard what Gray Fox promised. You know he will do as he says. Do you want to see your squaws and children die? If we try to keep on, it will happen."

He looked around the small circle, stifling argument with the power of his eyes. "None of you can say that what we've had is not bad. There comes a time when a man can no longer endure more. I say that time has come."

Again, Geronimo looked slowly about the circle, and fierce eyes dropped to the ground. All the arguing was done. In the morning he would tell Gray Fox that they would return with him to the reservation.

Crook hadn't slept well. It showed in his eyes. He waved aside all breakfast except coffee. Owen remembered the pressure from Washington Crook had spoken of. It must have been extremely bad. He had never seen the general as tense as that. Crook had accepted surrenders before, and he had been placidly calm. This time, he was different.

"They're coming," Crook announced. He peered at the approaching Apaches as though trying to read what was in their minds.

He shook his head, looked at Owen, and said abruptly, "Let's get it over with."

The talk went on and on, though Owen had

the feeling Geronimo intended to surrender. Geronimo had the Indian's love of talk, and he went over and over what had been discussed yesterday.

Crook wearied of it. "You know what you're going to do," he said flatly. "We have talked enough."

A brief flare of resistance appeared in Geronimo's eyes, then he seemed to cave in inwardly. "We accept," he said mournfully. "But there is one more thing I would like to ask. We would like to follow the Army in and not be surrounded."

Owen understood that was the last vestige of Geronimo's pride asking this concession. Geronimo wanted to cling to the last illusion that he was coming in undefeated.

Give him that, Owen prayed of Crook.

"Accepted," Crook said. "The march will start this morning."

He stood, watching Geronimo and the others ride away. "Better than I hoped for," he muttered. "Lieutenant, stay here and see that they start. I'm going on ahead to get the news off to Sheridan."

Owen did not smile, though he wanted to. Crook wanted to get the pressure from Washington stopped as quickly as he could.

"Bring them in to Bowie," Crook said and strode toward his mule.

The Apaches would need a little time to break

their camp, but Owen didn't mind that. This time, the waiting wouldn't be so hard.

"A white-eye's tent up ahead," Chihuahua said as he rode with Geronimo. "It was not here earlier."

Geronimo studied the tent. "No," he agreed. He stared at the figure before it. "It is Tribollet," he said. "The whisky seller."

Just the thought of whisky made the saliva start in his mouth. It had been a long time since he had had a drink, even of tiswin. "We see if he has whisky," he said suddenly. Surely at such a bad time, he should be allowed a few drinks to lighten his heavy heart.

Tribollet greeted Geronimo boisterously. "Ho, chief," he said, waving the demijohn he held. "The first drink for all your warriors is on me."

Geronimo accepted the offer. He had dealt with Tribollet before. A free drink was a rare offer.

The first demijohn was quickly emptied. The liquor spread warm and comforting in Geronimo's belly. The free whisky was all gone. It did not matter. The Apaches had money.

Tribollet brought out more demijohns. With each drink, Geronimo grew more garrulous. "I go back with Gray Fox because he promises me things will be better. The Apaches will no longer be cheated."

Tribollet shook his head sorrowfully. "I hate to tell you this, Geronimo. But you are being tricked. There is much talk among the soldiers that all Apaches will be killed the minute they step across the border. If not that, you will be moved to Florida, never to see Arizona again."

Geronimo stared at him, his eyebrows knitting together. "This is not true," he stated. His mind reeled. But why would Tribollet lie to him? Tribollet had nothing to gain.

Tribollet shook his head in pity. "It is true," he insisted. "Crook is tired of chasing you all over Mexico. He has been heard to say it will never happen again."

Geronimo took another long pull at the demijohn. His head felt light, his feet unsteady, but he could still reason. Crook had never tricked him before, but this was an old pattern. Why shouldn't Crook be like all the other white-eyes?

"I do not return," he said passionately. "I will live in peace. I go back into Mexico. Let the soldiers try to find me in the mountains of Sonora."

Tribollet grinned as he watched the heated discussion among the Apaches. He had done better than a fair job earning the money Mundane had promised him.

Not all of the Apaches agreed with Geronimo. They had listened to Gray Fox's words and were convinced. Geronimo was wrong.

Geronimo's band split up in two factions. Geronimo and thirty-seven people, nineteen of them warriors, turned south. The others rode north to where the Army waited.

Owen felt as though he had been hit in the stomach when he heard the news. None of the renegade Apaches would say why it had happened. Geronimo had just changed his mind. He and nineteen warriors were on the run again.

Oh God, Owen thought. This will crush Crook. He dreaded the prospects of having to tell the old man this shattering news. He sent two troopers to ride as fast as they could to catch Crook. It would be up to him to bring the remaining Apaches in.

"Lieutenant Maus," he said. "Take twenty troopers and thirty scouts with you. See if you can cut Geronimo's trail. If you catch up with him, try to convince him how wrong he is."

Maus's eyebrows rose. "If I can't, what then? What if he won't listen?"

"Do what you have to," Owen snapped. If it meant killing the Apache leader, so be it. But one way or another, Maus must not lose Geronimo's trail.

# Chapter 14

Crook already had the news when Owen arrived at Bowie. Owen had never seen a man more possessed by rage. It was one of those quiet rages that ate a man alive.

"How many did Geronimo take with him?" Crook asked tight-lipped.

"Nineteen warriors," Owen replied. "Thirty-eight people in all." He waited for an explosion.

It didn't come. Crook was bleak-eyed, and one fist was clenched tightly. But he said calmly enough, "Josanie had fewer warriors than that."

Owen nodded. The less he had to say the better off he thought he would be.

When the explosion came, it was awesome. Crook strode about his office, and he outdid any mule-skinner in the language he used.

He finally ran down and asked, "Why? Why did he change his mind?"

"I don't know, sir. I talked to the ones who came in. If they knew why, none of them would say."

Crook drew a deep breath, and Owen waited for another outburst of cursing.

Instead, Crook said calmly, "All to be done over again. My God, does it never end? I wish I'd killed Geronimo when I had the opportunity."

His shoulders slumped, and he said wearily, "I guess I don't mean that. I never knew Geronimo to do something without reason."

Crook's eyes were quieter as he looked at Owen. Owen dared venture a question. "Does Washington know?"

That was the wrong question, for Crook cursed again. "They know. For the past two days, I've done nothing but wire Washington. General Sheridan is very displeased. He suggests my Apache Scouts conspired to let Geronimo escape."

That stung Crook deeply. The scouts were a product of his making. Bitterness rode Crook's face, making him look haggard. It looked as though he needed somebody to talk to, and the fact that Owen was only a lieutenant didn't seem to make any difference.

"General Sheridan points out to me that I have forty-six companies of infantry and forty companies of cavalry. He believes that is more than ample force to subdue a handful of hostiles."

"Good God," Owen said in outraged disbelief. "I wish—"

Crook stared at him. Owen cut off the remainder. Crook knew that Owen wished Sheridan had experienced some of the last campaign. But it wasn't the smartest of policies to criticize one general to another.

Crook went on in that grim tone, "Washington

also disapproves of the surrender terms I gave Geronimo and the others. They demand I immediately renegotiate with them." He threw up his hands. "But none of them tell me how I can find Geronimo in those Mexican mountains."

He resumed his pacing. "The only thing Washington will allow is unconditional surrender. The hostiles will be allowed their lives. No more."

Owen was appalled. "But, sir, you told Chihuahua that—"

"I know what I told him," Crook snapped. "Never in my life have I broken my word to an Apache. But this time—" He turned and marched to his desk. He sat down behind it, his face looking as though it was carved out of marble.

"I've spent eight years of the hardest work I ever knew in this department," he said slowly. "But if Washington is no longer satisfied—" He shook his head, as though finding the next words hard to say. "So I have asked to be relieved of my command."

"No," Owen burst out. He thought of all the other commanders over the Department of Arizona. Crook was the only one who could point to any success.

"Yes." Crook's voice sounded hollow. His attempt at a smile was ghastly. "They can accept or refuse it. We'll see what turns out, Lieutenant."

• • •

Two days later, Crook got his answer. His resignation was accepted, effective immediately. Crook's promise to the seventy-five Apaches who surrendered was ruled null and void. Chihuahua and his people were to be sent to Florida. They were to be put on the train without informing them Crook's promise was broken.

Owen stood beside Crook at Bowie Station, watching the Apaches being loaded on the train.

Crook turned to Owen as the train pulled out. "God help me, I didn't tell them they were never to come back. I couldn't."

Was that a suspicious sheen of moisture in Crook's eyes? Owen put it down to imagination.

"General Nelson Miles is to relieve me. Serve him as well as you have served me."

"Yes, sir," Owen said. He was sick inside. He started to salute Crook, and Crook waved it aside. Instead he reached out and wrung Owen's hand.

"Good luck, Lieutenant," he said.

"You, too, sir," Owen returned.

Crook turned and walked away. Owen was sure there was a stinging in his eyes. That wasn't the familiar figure he knew at all. This one's shoulders drooped, and the former brisk stride was gone. Crook had reached the end of his trail. The taste had to be bitter to him.

# Chapter 15

General Nelson Appleton Miles was an imposing figure of a man. His face was somewhat chubby, and the full brush mustache didn't do much to make him look stern. He looked slowly about the office at his assembled staff officers. Miles was in full-dress uniform, including epaulets, a sash across his tunic, and rows of medals pinned across his chest.

Owen almost snorted his derision. Miles even had a sword belted at his side. By God, Owen thought, a sword in Arizona! He couldn't help but contrast Miles's spit-and-polish look to Crook's rough appearance. His derision grew. On what little knowledge he had of Miles, he would predict Miles would never be out of uniform. Crook was seldom in one.

Miles wasn't a West Pointer, though from his appearance and manner, one might assume that he was. He had a well-earned reputation. Miles had fought the Kiowas, Comanches, and Cheyennes, and had seen long service against the Sioux. His greatest achievement was corralling Chief Joseph and the Nez Percé Indians.

All right, Owen admitted. Miles had experience in fighting Indians. But damn it, Miles knew nothing about the Apaches, and that was the glaring difference. He was up against an entirely different breed of Indians. Before, he had faced large, hostile numbers. Now, he had to pit an army against a handful of renegades, a small group of renegades that rarely left more tracks than a bird in the air. Owen knew he was prejudiced against the new general; he still rebelled over Crook's replacement. Give Miles a chance, he growled to himself.

Miles was all fire and brimstone. "Gentlemen, I have studied the difficulty. I am well aware of your problems. I believe your renegades have been given too much time. We will harass them constantly, give them no rest, allow them no hiding place. My policy is total extermination."

Owen didn't dare look at all the grave faces before Miles. These were experienced Apache hunters. It was a good thing Miles couldn't read their minds. What Miles spouted might sound good to Washington, but he was leaving out one important factor: Geronimo would have something to say about his resting and hiding places. He had the entire wilderness of the Sierra Madre to choose from.

"There will be no letup at any time," Miles went on. "I intend to keep a column of cavalry on every Apache trail that is found. If that column breaks down, another will immediately replace it."

Owen kept his face wooden. Miles made it

sound so goddamned easy, as though he was moving checkers on a board. If he kept making his moves, the one checker he wanted would be swept off the board.

Miles stared fiercely about at the faces in the room as though daring opposition. "We will not give Geronimo one hour to rest. That kind of pursuit will break him down. He will surrender, or he will die."

Nothing but empty words, Owen thought in disgust. Hadn't Crook followed much the same policy? Did the same words coming from a new general sound more impressive to Washington?

Miles briskly rubbed his hands together. "Five thousand soldiers in the Department of Arizona. Will anybody here dare tell me we haven't the tools to finish the job?"

Maybe we haven't, Owen thought sardonically. Maybe we need a little something more, such as a strong element of luck in locating Geronimo again.

Owen moodily watched the general. Miles talked about thirty-eight hostiles almost contemptuously. That wasn't even a good handful. All Miles had to do was to close his fingers. You'll learn, Owen thought savagely. Owen foresaw hard and difficult days ahead for the Army. Miles was driven by ambition. He would not allow Geronimo and that piddling handful of followers to blot his reputation.

Miles's eyes bored into Owen. "Lieutenant Parnell," he barked. "You have followed Geronimo longer than anybody else. Have you anything to add?"

Owen felt his cheeks burn. Miles was publicly pointing out his failure. Digging Geronimo out of Mexico and turning him back didn't mean a thing. Goddamn Geronimo, he thought with a renewed burst of passion. Geronimo's breaking back had knocked Crook out of the running. Miles seemed to have gone through the files thoroughly. Owen locked eyes with Miles and felt antagonism spring up between them. Did one recognize the moment when his career shattered? This could be such a time for him.

"No, sir," he said steadily. "Nothing to add."

He walked out with the other staff members, not daring to look back. He was quite sure Miles would be watching him.

Owen expected orders to take the field again. When they didn't come, he was sure that Miles was deliberately casting aside all Owen's experience, all of his personal knowledge of Geronimo. He wanted to rave and swear. Instead, he got quietly and thoroughly drunk that night.

Lieutenant Sam Gibson shook him awake in the morning. "It's after reveille, Owen. You trying to get in wrong with Miles?"

Owen sat up and groaned. An incautious move

would send his head tumbling off his shoulders.

Gibson smelled the air in the room and said, "Whew. It smells like a distillery in here. Drinking alone can be bad business."

Owen stood and walked unsteadily to a mirror. He shuddered at his reflection. His eyes were red-rimmed, his cheeks hollowed. "This morning, I believe you're right, Sam."

Gibson had come out of the Point four years after Owen's graduation. It struck Owen with peculiar force that Gibson was advancing faster than he was. Who isn't, he thought glumly.

Gibson sat down and watched Owen shave. He had a high good humor that was rarely disturbed. He also had a keen and perceptive mind.

"You and the old man at odds?" Gibson asked.

Owen finished scraping one cheek. "Does it show that much?"

"Ah," Gibson said softly. "Because of your close connections with Crook?"

Owen started to say that had to be it, then reconsidered. He shrugged and let the question go unanswered.

"It's a criminal shame," Gibson burst out. "There's not another man who knows Geronimo better."

"Go tell Miles that," Owen growled.

Gibson shuddered. "He'd hand me my head."

Owen realized Gibson was watching him closely. So Gibson did have a reason for awakening him this morning. "What is it, Sam?" he asked impatiently.

"Geronimo and Nachez hit a ranch in Santa Cruz Valley yesterday. They killed a cowboy and some of Peck's family." He shook his head in unconscious admiration. "Geronimo took a chance in ducking back into Arizona."

Geronimo had no other alternative, Owen thought. The ranches in Mexico were poor and widely spaced. The frantic need for supplies and fresh horses had driven Geronimo into this desperate foray.

Owen's face was frozen as he remembered other attacked ranches he had seen. The Santa Cruz Valley was just this side of the border.

"Miles didn't remove Crook's border patrols, did he?"

"He doesn't talk to a lieutenant," Gibson jeered. "He could have. He's made a lot of changes."

Owen slashed the air with the edge of his palm. Miles had made changes, such as dismissing most of Crook's Apache Scouts. Without them, how did Miles expect to keep on Geronimo's trail?

"Geronimo got away?" Owen asked.

"Maybe not," Gibson said. "Captain Lebo and his company were in the vicinity."

Lebo was the able commander of Company K of the Tenth Cavalry. Most of his troop were seasoned in the campaign against Victorio six years earlier.

“We’ll see what happens,” Owen grunted. He wasn’t unduly optimistic. He had seen too many other men go out after Geronimo and return empty-handed and worn out.

The days dragged by, and reports of Lebo’s pursuit came in with maddening slowness. The lack of even fragmentary reports told Owen that Lebo had to be deep into Mexico. He could also tell how Lebo’s pursuit was going by the expression on Miles’s face whenever he saw him. The first days after the reported contact with Geronimo, Miles had looked confident, almost cocky.

You’ll see, Owen silently promised Miles. Maybe the thought was even tinged with malice. Geronimo wouldn’t be run to earth in a few days, or even weeks. Owen had no reason to assume this pursuit would be any different than all the others.

The absence of reports must have been driving Miles wild, for each passing day changed his expression. His cheeks tightened, and his lip thinned. Miles was learning the hard way, Owen thought. He was learning some of the frustration Crook had known.

Each day, Owen prayed that Miles would send him into the field. Not that he thought he could do any better, but the life of a postbound officer was driving him crazy. He couldn’t help but think of the last exchange of words he had had with Mundane. He had derisively pointed out to Mundane that he was a desk officer. He should have been more sympathetic to the man.

Owen thought often of Stella, even to the extent of writing her several letters. But he tore up all of them except one—a stiff little note, stating that he was busy and unable to ride into Tucson. He considered adding "I miss you" but decided against it.

He walked into the orderly room and put his letter to Stella with the dispatches going to Fort Lowell. He hoped somebody would take it on to Tucson. His head jerked about as he heard Miles's voice coming from the inner office.

"You will leave in the morning, Lieutenant Gibson," Miles said crisply.

Owen knew a sour envy of Gibson. He didn't know what duty was being assigned Gibson, but anything would be preferable to post duty.

"Give Captain Lebo all the assistance necessary," Miles went on.

"Yes, sir," Gibson replied.

Owen walked out of the office, sick with boredom and frustration. Gibson had the assignment that should have been given him.

He was out early in the morning to see Gibson leave with Troop B of the Fourth Cavalry. He reached up and shook Gibson's hand.

"Good luck, Sam," he said and meant it. He

didn't add, keep your eyes open, though it loomed big in his mind. If Sam didn't know that already, God help him.

He watched the cavalry canter away. Mentally, he would be with Gibson every step of the way. Waiting to hear of any progress would be long and hard to bear. Where Gibson was going, he wouldn't be near a telegraph pole.

The days picked up their dreary parade. One day was like the one that preceded it until Owen wanted to yell against the oppressive monotony.

By the calendar, it wasn't a long space of time, but Owen was sure he had aged immeasurably when a report finally came in from Lebo.

Owen didn't hear the report firsthand; Miles wouldn't allow him that privilege. But Owen didn't care how many hands the report passed through. After chasing Geronimo some two hundred miles, Lebo had made contact with the Indian band in the Pinito Mountains. After a brief skirmish that cost Lebo one killed and one wounded, the Indians had broken off and disappeared. Lebo's horses were in such bad shape that he couldn't continue the pursuit. He was being relieved by Lieutenant Gibson. Now there would be more of that maddening waiting until Gibson reported.

Owen saw Miles's face grow haggard as the days lengthened into weeks, then months. That pompous assurance was all gone, and Miles's face grew strained and careworn.

Suffer, you bastard, Owen thought. Now you're beginning to realize what Crook went through.

Half a hundred times, Owen was tempted to resign his commission, but a queer pride held him steady. He was available, though Miles didn't use him, except on routine patrols. Owen covered mile after mile, checking on heliograph stations on prominent mountain peaks. This was another of Miles's innovations, and Owen sourly regarded the thirty-odd heliograph posts established in Arizona and New Mexico as a waste of time and manpower.

He found the same boredom growing in the small detachments assigned to guard the heliographs. In theory, the plan was fine. The bright sunlight and clear air enabled messages to be transmitted rapidly, but the posts weren't where Geronimo was. Geronimo was deep in Sonora, Mexico. This wasn't a new idea. The Apache had used the same system long ago, but they used smoke signals.

Owen completed his swing of inspection of the heliograph posts and returned to Bowie. His mind was almost made up. He was doing no good here. Any noncommissioned officer could accomplish what he was doing. He would march into Miles's office when he returned and resign. He felt an empty sickness, but his decision was made.

He dismounted at Bowie and handed over the reins to the sergeant in charge of the stable area.

"Lieutenant Gibson just got in, sir," the sergeant said.

"Is he all right?" Owen asked with a quick, revived interest.

"Pretty beat up, sir." He answered Owen's unspoken question. "Geronimo's still on the run."

Owen hurried to find Gibson. Gibson was seated in a tub of water when Owen entered his room. The bright good humor and the spark in Gibson's eyes were gone. How well Owen knew how he felt—physically spent with the crushing burden of failure pressing him down more.

Gibson tried to grin at Owen and failed. "I chased him four months, Owen, with not a goddamned thing to show for it."

"Four months?" Owen said in appalled astonishment. He knew the days had been turning to weeks, but he hadn't realized so much time had passed.

"You never saw Geronimo, Sam?"

For a moment, Gibson thought that was censure in Owen's tone, for he frowned. Then his face cleared. Owen wasn't criticizing him; he only wanted information.

"Twice, we caught fleeting glimpses of Apaches. At times, I was positive we were chasing mountain goats. You wouldn't believe the country Geronimo led us through."

"I can believe," Owen said quietly. "Go on."

"In one day, I lost three of my sixteen mules over the side of a mountain." Gibson's eyes were shadowed with the memory. "When a mule can't hold its feet, nothing can. The few Indian trackers I had with me finally gave up and refused to look any more."

"Miles should have kept the scouts," Owen said angrily.

"Don't you think I know that?" Gibson asked. "I don't blame my trackers for quitting. Those miles of rock finally whipped them."

Gibson was silent a long moment, then he sighed. "That red devil used every trick I ever heard of, some I didn't know. He set a fire to hide his tracks. We ran for a solid half day to get out of a forest fire. When we got out of that, the only thing we were thinking of was water. We found it a day later." Gibson threw up his hands in despair. "We were through then. I ruined a lot of horses and men, Owen."

"I know," Owen soothed him. Hadn't he gone through the same thing? Gibson was suffering with his failure, and Owen hated to ask him the next question. He wouldn't blame Gibson for not wanting to talk about it anymore.

"What about Geronimo?" he asked.

Gibson grimaced. It was a much milder reaction than Owen expected.

"The last I heard of him he was still down in

the Sierra Madres." He stood and reached for a towel. He looked with distaste at the filthy water in the tub. A little thicker and it could be called mud.

"I didn't think I'd ever get clean again," he said as he dried himself. "If we weren't traveling over solid rock, it was a pulverized dust that rose in a constant cloud. A man breathed it until he could taste nothing else. Men and animals sweated, and the dust stuck to it, forming a solid crust. I didn't think I'd ever see enough water to wash in again."

"Is anybody on Geronimo's trail, Sam?" Owen asked impatiently.

"What trail?" Gibson jeered. He relented at the heat in Owen's expression. "Captain Lawton is supposed to be. He had his special unit with him."

"Ah," Owen said softly. That special unit was another of Miles's innovations. Owen had watched it forming with interest. From all over the Department of Arizona, Miles had gathered the trained athletes of his command. Lawton was a prime example of those hundred men. He was six-four, and if there ever was a man physically fit, he was one. Miles's theory was that a trained athlete would more than outdo the Apache in endurance.

Owen wouldn't argue with that; not yet. But it had to be proven. He contrasted Lawton's bulk against the small, wiry Apaches. He was afraid that physical fitness alone wasn't the answer. It took cunning, an innate knowledge of how to survive in this brutal country. A man learned that by living a lifetime in it, not by merely building up his muscles.

Owen's face was heavy with concentration. Geronimo had been running for a long time. So far, he had shown no indication of weakening. Maybe Lawton could bring him to bay, but Owen had his doubts. Personally, he would rather have the Apache Scouts than Lawton's unit. Fight fire with fire was still a pretty good adage.

Gibson finished drying himself and reached for his drawers. "Do you think Lawton can do it, Owen?"

"I don't know," Owen said soberly. "Lawton had better turn in some positive results, and soon, or Miles will go crazy. The newspapers are beginning to ride him pretty hard for his lack of success. The news accounts are comparing him unfavorably to Crook. Some of them are openly stating that Arizona was far better off when Crook was in command."

He paused, then asked, "Have you reported to Miles yet, Sam?"

Gibson looked as though he had bitten into something bad. "You don't know how much I dreaded that, Owen." His face darkened at the memory. "I thought he was going to bite my head off. I wish to God he'd been along." He grinned sheepishly. "Forget I said that."

"Sure," Owen agreed. He could appreciate Gibson's outburst. Failure was bad enough to stand without being raked over the coals for it.

"I rode in today with my mind fully made up to resign my commission, Sam."

Before the shock could fully register on Gibson's face, Owen said, "But I changed my mind. I'm getting worse than a woman. Now, I think I'll stick around and see how Lawton makes out." Perhaps he was vindicative in the petty satisfaction he felt. Miles's glory trail had turned into a vicious animal. Miles had it by the tail and couldn't let go.

"You think Washington kicked out the wrong man, don't you?" Gibson asked.

"I know it," Owen said firmly.

# Chapter 16

Survivors from Lawton's expedition began trickling back to Bowie. It didn't mean that Lawton's unit was wiped out, but these men were casualties. Owen talked to as many of them as he could. These were the walking wounded, though there was no evidence of outward injury—the wounds were in the spirit. He talked to big, powerful men worn down to shadows of their former selves. Their hands did not shake, and there was no trembling in them, but that once-supreme inner confidence had been lost on Geronimo's trail. Their bone-deep exhaustion dulled their eyes, and something they couldn't understand had shattered their spirits.

Sergeant Barnes was the most articulate, and Owen talked to him for a long time.

He was only a husk of the old Barnes. His feet were bandaged, and there were haunted shadows in his eyes.

"I volunteered for Lawton's unit," he said. "I welcomed a chance to get away from the monotony of post life. I'd never do it again."

Those past months were too vivid in Barnes's mind. Owen waited for him to go on.

There was no embarrassment in the man's manner. He had been up against something he couldn't cope with, and he admitted it simply. "I knew there was no man in the world who could outride, or outwalk me. I was wrong. Every brave in Geronimo's bunch can outdo me. He led us up one mountain and down another until I was convinced I'd never see another level stretch of ground."

His eyes pleaded for understanding, and Owen nodded. He knew what Barnes was talking about. He'd been there.

"We followed him into the Dragoon Mountains. He even got fairly close to Fort Apache. It looked like he might've been trying to get to some of his people for help. Captain Lawton thought we had him then. But Geronimo turned and ducked back into Mexico. My God, I couldn't believe he'd go back into that hell. I guess that's what whipped me. What the hell are those bastards made of?"

Owen offered Barnes papers and a sack of tobacco. Barnes waved aside the offer and bit off a chew of tobacco.

"They're made out of pure rawhide," Owen said. "How did Captain Lawton take it?"

"Hard, like the rest of us," Barnes grunted. "He was the toughest-looking man I'd ever seen. He never quit, just wore out. He got to the point when he could no longer pull himself into his saddle. I was there when he couldn't make it and just slumped to the ground. I swear there were tears in his eyes. He had to be carried in a travois to stay with the troop. But he's still out there. He's a better man than I am." Barnes waved at his bandaged feet. "It got to the point where I couldn't go another step." There was no shame in his eyes.

Owen felt no criticism of him. There came a moment when a man's spirit could no longer go on. Tired and aching muscles were bad enough, but they could still be forced on by an indomitable will. But when the spirit was beaten, he was through.

Barnes was silent, picking at the memories that were burned deep into his brain. "I looked like a damned ragpicker when I finally got here. Nobody would have known I was an American soldier by the way I looked. My boot soles were gone, and my feet were blistered and swollen. The rock cuts were bad enough, but the damned cactus spines festered. I'm still not getting around too well." He spat at a cuspidor, and the metal pinged softly. "Walking got hard enough, but to add to the general misery, a lot of us got diarrhea. It was as close to hell as I ever want to get." A brief shudder ran through him. "Those redskins aren't human."

"It seems that way," Owen agreed wryly.

"All that effort for nothing," Barnes muttered. "Lieutenant, we didn't accomplish a damned thing."

"Yes, you did," Owen disagreed. "Geronimo

covered every mile you did. He has to be just as tired; he has to be hurting. You may not believe it, but even an Apache has his limit of endurance." A thought struck him, and he asked, "Sergeant, which men gave out first, the big brawny ones, or the smaller, wiry ones?"

"The bigger ones every time," Barnes responded. "It burned hell out of me to know I was giving out, and a few little scrawny bastards kept right on going. Ah," he said, as the meaning of Owen's question hit him. "It looks like Miles should have picked men built like the Apaches."

Owen smiled and stood. "Something like that." Another one of Miles's high-flying plans was shot full of holes. He was too conceited to use the methods that had brought Crook success. It seemed that he couldn't learn by another man's experience. He had to learn by his own mistakes. Owen forced the thoughts away. He was turning into an irascible old man.

"Let me know if you need anything, Sergeant."

"Can't think of anything, Lieutenant. They treat me real good. All I want now is just to lay here for the next six months."

Owen laughed. "Then I hope you get your wish."

He walked out of the hospital and turned towards headquarters. He knew for sure now what he was going to do. He was going to march into Miles's office and resign.

A corporal found him before he was halfway to headquarters. "My God, Lieutenant, where have you been? I've been looking all over for you. The general wants to see you."

"Then we want to see each other," Owen said. He didn't know why Miles wanted him and didn't care. His spirits were higher than they had been for many a week.

He walked into Miles's office and saluted. "Lieutenant Parnell reporting as requested, sir," he said woodenly. Maybe he had a vindictive streak in him. He would wait until Miles assigned him another piddling chore, then throw it back into his face.

Miles looked bad. When a man lost his assurance, it showed in his face. The general's eyes were harried, and his face looked strained.

"Sit down, Lieutenant," Miles said.

Owen's interest sharpened at the conciliatory tone in Miles's voice. He sat down, his eyes alert. Miles had something on his mind that he was finding hard to say. Owen waited easily, letting Miles fumble ahead without assistance.

Miles kept his eyes fastened on papers on his desk as he talked. "Lieutenant, I heard that you probably know Geronimo better than any other officer in my command."

It was a distinction Owen hadn't thought of before, but with Crawford dead and Crook gone, Miles could be right. He still couldn't see what

Miles was driving at, and he said cautiously, "I've talked to him, General."

Miles looked squarely at Owen for the first time, and his eyes were sick. "I've heard a report from Mexico that Geronimo is talking to the prefect at Fronteras about a possible surrender to the Mexican government. That would be a foolish thing for him to do. He should know he can't trust the Mexicans. With the hatred that exists between them—" Miles made a vague gesture and didn't finish.

Owen almost snorted. He could read Miles's thoughts as plainly as though they were written out. If Geronimo surrendered to the Mexicans, there went Miles's glory. Miles was finally convinced that he couldn't beat Geronimo with military force. It had to be done with the method Crook had used. He had to reason with Geronimo, to talk him into surrendering.

"What does the general have in mind?" Owen asked smoothly. There was that vindictive streak showing again. He wanted to see Miles squirm a little more.

The frantic tone in Miles's voice increased. "Lieutenant, I thought if you could talk to him and show him where he's making a serious mistake, show him that he would be separated forever from his relatives and friends, it may change his thinking."

How badly Owen wanted to throw Miles's

words back into his face. He thought of all the effort, all the hardship that had gone before, and withheld his indignant words. He owed Grimes, Crawford, and Crook something, didn't he? Yes, and even himself.

"I'll let you pick the men you wish to accompany you," Miles said desperately. "Twenty-five of the best soldiers in all of Arizona—" He stared astounded at the lieutenant. Owen was shaking his head.

"I don't want a military escort, General. I couldn't get close to Geronimo with a fighting force. I'll pick the few men I want to go with me."

For a moment, the old hauteur filled Miles's eyes, then the last resistance collapsed. "As you think best, Lieutenant. All I want you to do is to arrange for me to talk to Geronimo."

"I would like a written order from you, sir, ordering any command I might run across to give me whatever assistance I might need. But I will have the final decision."

Miles locked eyes with him, then sighed. He wrote rapidly on a piece of paper, then handed it to Owen. "I think that will do it, Lieutenant." He didn't look at Owen as he muttered, "I wish you all the luck in the world."

I'll bet you do, Owen thought sardonically. "Yes, sir," he said, tucking the piece of paper in his shirt pocket.

He saluted and walked out of the office. “You’re out of your goddamned head,” he swore. It was starting all over again, and he had asked to be thrown back squarely into the middle of the mess.

# Chapter 17

At Fort Apache, Owen picked five men to go with him: two of the original scouts, Chatto and Martín; and George Wratten to interpret, Frank Huston as packer, and Tex Whaley as a courier. All of them were reluctant at first, but they finally consented to go. Wratten put it well: "If you think there's a chance, then it's got to be done. It's about time somebody stopped this madness."

Chatto put it more succinctly. He looked long at Owen, then shook his head. "You crazy in the head," he said.

Owen grinned. "I've already told myself that. You want the fighting ended, don't you?"

"Yes," Chatto said vehemently, displaying a rare emotion. "Best for everybody."

Owen picked the best riding mules he could find. Crook would have approved of that. He contrasted this tiny train with all the other pack trains that had headed into Mexico. This one didn't measure up in any way. He wasn't planning on a long expedition. He wanted to get into Mexico and find Geronimo as quickly as possible. That was optimistic, but he wouldn't allow himself to consider any other outcome.

"Where we headed for?" Wratten asked.

“Fronteras. That’s the last place Geronimo was heard of.”

Wratten’s glum face shouted as plainly as though he yelled it. Fronteras was a hell of a long way.

The days fell away and piled up like dying leaves dropping from a tree in the fall. Owen tried to keep his mind closed to everything but the day ahead. Each day was filled with the same drab monotony. The summer sun blazed fiercely, forcing Owen to start long before dawn and keep moving until the heat drove them to seek whatever shade they could find. Then he would start out shortly before sundown, pushing on into the cooler hours. It didn’t leave many hours to sleep, for he was riding through the bearable ones. They might rest through the middle of the day, but sleep was almost impossible for anybody.

The little band made seventy miles the last day and camped outside of Fronteras. It was a sad little Mexican town, but Owen was surprised to find it as large as it was. How could people live in such a country?

He went into town to replenish supplies, knowing that, even though they would be scanty and of poor quality, whatever he could buy would be better than what they had lived on for the past week. Ground corn thickened with molasses into a mush made sorry eating.

Owen was startled to run into Lieutenant Wilder. Wilder's being here meant that he, too, had heard Geronimo was in this vicinity. Owen's disappointment was at first hard to swallow, then he knew relief. Let Wilder reach Geronimo first. Owen didn't want the glory.

Wilder shook his head at Owen's words. "My command's shot, Owen. We can't go another mile until we rest. I sent a runner to Captain Lawton. He should join me in a few days. Besides, I wouldn't know Geronimo if he came up and spit in my face. If anybody's going to talk to him, you're the one."

Owen sighed and accepted the odious burden. "Any news of Geronimo?"

"I talked to two of his squaws a couple of days ago," Wilder answered. "He sent them in to talk surrender to the prefect. They wouldn't listen to me about surrendering to the American government. They would only do what Geronimo told them. There's something in the air, all right. The prefect sent the squaws back with three horses loaded with food and supplies." Wilder paused and squinted at Owen. "That third horse was loaded with mescal."

"What the hell's he doing sending mescal to Geronimo?" Owen exploded.

"Maybe the prefect is getting cute," Wilder drawled. "If he can get Geronimo drunk enough, it would make it a lot easier to kill him and his bunch. The town's been loading up with Mexican soldiers. It all ties together, doesn't it?"

"It does," Owen snapped. "Geronimo won't fall for that. The Mexicans have tried to get him drunk before." Just the same, he was worried. He wanted to see Geronimo off the warpath, but he didn't want to see it done by deceit and outright murder.

"Do you happen to know which way those squaws went?"

"East," Wilder replied promptly. "The prefect is pretty unhappy about American soldiers being down here. He'd like to order all of us out, but that would be disobeying the governor of Sonora. But I don't think you'll be able to follow those squaws. The prefect's soldiers would stop you before you got very far."

Owen looked at the setting sun. He still had some daylight left. "I'll go south far enough to mislead the prefect. Then I'll swing east and see if we can't pick up the squaws' trail."

"I'm glad it's you and not me. Watch yourself, Owen."

"You can bet on that. If anything happens, I'll try to send a runner back to let you know."

"I'll hold Lawton here," Wilder said. He wrung Owen's hand hard.

Owen headed south, watching his back trail. For several miles, he was sure he was being followed. Wratten was watching the back trail, too. After four or five miles, he grunted, "Looks like they dropped off, Owen. Maybe we convinced them we're heading in the wrong direction."

"We'll sleep a few hours," Owen replied, "then swing east and see if we can pick up the squaws' trail."

Martín and Chatto found the tracks in the morning with no difficulty. "Two squaws," Chatto announced. "Three horses."

"Let's get on with it," Owen said impatiently. He felt tight inside. Each step carried them deeper into hostile country. He thought of Wilder's and Lawton's commands. He wished both of them were around him.

At the end of the three days, the tracks were fresh. Owen followed them down the Bavispe River and made camp at the base of a mountain. Every instinct told him that Geronimo was very near.

He stood, conferring with Chatto and Martín. "Tracks go up mountain," Chatto grunted. "I think Geronimo is watching us right now."

That crawling feeling was along Owen's spine again. Every instinct agreed with Chatto.

"Do you think he'd let me ride up there?"

Chatto soberly shook his head. "He'd shoot any white-eye that dared get close." He sucked in a deep breath as he made his decision. "Me and Martín go up there and tell Geronimo Bse-chee Day-son wants to talk to him."

Hearing the Apache name for Big Nose almost made Owen smile. "Maybe he won't talk to you, either."

Martín nodded without answering. Both scouts were well aware of that possibility. Martín laid his rifle on the ground and Chatto followed suit.

A flicker of a smile touched Chatto's lips. "Two rifles do no good now."

Owen watched them make their way slowly up the mountain. It would be a hell of a time waiting until he heard from them again.

# Chapter 18

The sun had covered only a small slice of the arc of the sky, but to the waiting man it seemed as though a whole season had passed. Owen didn't realize how tense he was until he saw Chatto coming back down the mountain.

Owen rushed up to meet him. "Where is Martín?" Chatto's grin was due more to relief than merriment.

"With Geronimo." He pointed toward the crest. "Up there. Most of the way we felt rifles covering us. It is strange thing to sweat so hard and feel so cold. Martín's cousin is one of Geronimo's warriors. I think that is the reason they did not shoot us. It is good you sent only two; more would not have survived. We told Geronimo you want to talk about possible surrender. He will see you. I take you to the place Geronimo selected to talk. Do not bring others. Geronimo suspicious of everything."

"He knows I don't have many men," Owen grunted, but he accepted Geronimo's restrictions and understood his suspicions.

Chatto guided Owen to the meeting-place in the nearby bend of the Bavispe River. Wood, grass, and shade were plentiful. Owen stopped Chatto just outside of the selected spot and rode on ahead, carrying a flag of truce. He dismounted and unsaddled his horse. He threw his saddle on the ground and laid his pistol and carbine across it, then moved away from the saddle and stood waiting.

Each passing minute seemed to stretch into eons. Then Geronimo's warriors drifted in like shadows. That coldness crawled over Owen's spine again. Once, he had talked to most of these braves on a friendly basis, but that basis did not exist now. Their eyes glittered coldly as they watched him. Owen was relieved to see Martín with them.

Geronimo was the last to arrive. He laid his Winchester on the ground. "Ho, Bse-chee Dayson," he greeted. The greeting did not extend to his eyes. He grinned faintly. "It has been a long time since we have talked."

"Too long, Geronimo," Owen said earnestly. "I wanted to stop you from making a foolish move."

Geronimo's eyebrows rose in surprise. "I do not make foolish moves." Stiffness was in his voice.

"You may be making one now," Owen said. "The prefect sent you much mescal. Did you know he is also gathering many soldiers to kill you?"

Geronimo chuckled derisively. "I know. We drank his mescal. Ah, it was a glorious drunk." His tone was wistful. "But it did not make me lay down my caution." He snorted. "I know the

Mexicans too well. Do you think they could have surprised me?"

"No," Owen said simply.

Geronimo held out a shaky hand. "I need a drink." His face lighted with hope. "Do you have whisky?"

Owen shook his head. "No, but we may have a little tobacco."

"That would help," Geronimo said eagerly.

"May I send Chatto back to my camp to bring it here?" Owen suggested.

"Bring your entire party," Geronimo granted. "It is small."

Owen sent Chatto to bring up the other men. He gathered what tobacco he had and passed it around. Apaches and whites sat around, smoking cigarettes rolled in corn husks.

"I am tired," Geronimo said abruptly. "I have traveled too far. I am lonely to see my family and friends. What have you to say?"

"I never lied to you," Owen said slowly.

Geronimo reflected on this, then bobbed his head. "No, you never have. You and Gray Fox were the only white-eyes I believed. Now he is gone."

"He is gone," Owen agreed. "What he promised you can no longer stand."

Alarm flickered in Geronimo's eyes. "All I ask is the original terms. We will return to San Carlos and resume our farming. We expect our usual rations and no punishment for what we have done."

Owen shook his head, almost sadly. "I could lie to you and agree, but I cannot. Things have changed. Your friends and people are no longer in Arizona. They have been moved to Florida. To join them, you must go there."

A murmur of disagreement rose from the listening warriors, sounding like the sough of a winter wind through tree branches.

Geronimo was stunned. It showed in his harsh suck of breath. "If I do not agree?"

"Then the war goes on until finally the last of your band is dead. That is inevitable. You and I know it. Two governments hunt you. Do you think you can avoid both governments forever?"

Geronimo's mouth thinned, and that old angry glare showed in his eyes. "I have done well so far."

"But each passing day adds its weight," Owen pointed out. "You said you are tired. The weariness will only grow more. You never will know another minute of peace. Can a man sleep well with that on his shoulders?"

Geronimo stared at the ground and muttered so low that Owen could not make out his words.

Owen had no idea of how Geronimo would react. The Apache could be building up a rage that would prompt him to blot out his tormentor.

But Owen had chosen a path, and he plowed doggedly ahead.

"There comes a time when a man comes up against a wall that he cannot climb or go around. What does he do—retrace his steps, or wait helplessly until the wall falls and crushes him? All Chiricahua and Warm Springs Apaches will be moved to join Chihuahua and the ones who were moved with him. If you could stay in Arizona, you would have to live among the White Mountain, Aravapia, and all other hostile Apache tribes. They are your traditional enemies. You are few. Do you think you could live in peace with them?"

Geronimo's face showed nothing, but his eyes were harried. He stood abruptly and said, "We will meet in the morning. My people and I must talk." He stalked off, and the warriors rose and followed him.

Wratten's exhalation of breath was a ragged sound. "What do you think, Owen?"

Owen shrugged. "He knows I've never lied to him. That's in our favor. What other course does he have?" One powerful factor was in their favor—Geronimo, by his own admission, was tired. The rigors of all those months of running showed plainly.

He sighed and said, "We'll just have to wait until morning. Maybe we'd better do a little praying."

"I have been ever since we got here," Wratten said. "I never sweated so much in my life."

Owen grinned. "I know. And it all starts over tomorrow. After their talk tonight, they could be so enraged that they'd want to wipe us out."

"My God, you sure give a man pleasant dreams," Wratten said sourly.

"Don't I?" Owen agreed and laughed.

Owen and his party moved back to their original camp and waited for the morning. They talked late into the night, and after that Owen could sleep little. He wondered if the Apaches were sleeping any better.

Geronimo and the others were at the appointed meeting spot early in the morning. Owen couldn't read a thing in those surly faces. The sweating Wratten spoke of started all over again.

"What kind of a man is your new Big Chief?" was Geronimo's first question. "He is like Gray Fox?"

"Not like Gray Fox," Owen said cautiously. "But what promises he makes will be kept."

Geronimo's sigh came deep from his chest. "He has to be a good man, or the Great Father would not have sent him. I want to talk to him before we make our final decision."

Owen frowned, and Geronimo said, "Perhaps he will modify the terms. Perhaps he will make them less harsh." Owen started to speak, and

Geronimo motioned him quiet. "If you were an Apache, what would you advise me to do?"

Owen kept his face blank. "If I walked in your moccasins, I would accept, as the terms are now. I would think only of saving my people's lives."

Geronimo seemed to wilt. "I follow your advice. We ride to meet your Captain Lawton." A small smile touched his face. "He is near us." He paused and said reflectively, "It will be our first meeting. Your captain has never seen me, though I have looked on him from afar. He is a determined man."

At Owen's startled look, Geronimo grinned. "Ho, did you think we did not know where your people were?"

"We ride to meet him," Owen said. The surrender wasn't yet accomplished, but the hardest step, the first one, was taken.

It took a full day of riding to reach Lawton's camp. Captain Lawton came out to meet Geronimo. Owen was shocked at Lawton's appearance, remembering how he looked before he left Bowie. The muscles were still there, but they were stringy and wasted. His body was emaciated, and his face was lined and haggard.

Lawton looked critically at Geronimo, then a small smile twitched at his lip corners. "You ran my ass off," he said.

Wratten interpreted Lawton's words. Geronimo broke into a cackle of laughter. "Tell the captain he has a very thick ass to take so much wearing down. No other man could have pushed us so hard and long."

Lawton broke into laughter and thrust out his hand. Geronimo took it, his face wreathed in smiles. Owen was well aware of the respect these two had for each other.

Geronimo still would not surrender to Lawton. That troubled Lawton, and he talked it over at length with Owen.

Owen tried to ease his concern, "Geronimo will only surrender to Miles. Geronimo is a chieftain. He thinks it only proper to surrender to another chieftain."

Lawton was dubious. "Do you really think that?"

"I do," Owen assured him.

Lawton pulled at his fingers. "I guess we have to wait for Miles to ride down and meet us. God knows how long that will take."

"Miles knows that Geronimo is coming in?" Owen asked.

Lawton's expression didn't lighten. "He should by now. I sent runners to the nearest wire."

"I pray to God Miles doesn't fiddle around," Owen said. At Lawton's frown, he explained. "If he takes too long to talk to Geronimo, it could be considered an insult. We're still in Mexico. If Geronimo gets impatient—" He shrugged. "I don't know what he will do then."

Lawton groaned. "If Geronimo breaks on me like he did Crook, Miles will skin me." He stared blackly at a campfire.

Miles probably would, Owen thought. If that should happen, it could shatter Lawton's career. Owen felt pity for him. Worry was a constant torment to a man who clung to the glory trail.

"I've got half a mind to arrest all of them and put them under guard," Lawton muttered.

"Don't even think of it," Owen said sharply. The two camps were a good mile apart. Any overt move from Lawton toward the Apache camp would alert Geronimo. "You wouldn't make a hundred yards without starting a fight. You've got the numbers, but that's no guarantee of your winning. If Geronimo slips away again, where would that leave you?"

Lawton looked stricken at the thought. "You're right," he agreed. "I've lost too many good men as it is. Damn it, if I could only get this over with."

"We all want it over," Owen said. "But one wrong move could wreck everything. Don't let that happen."

"I won't," Lawton said. He grinned twistedly. "When a man gets so tired, he quits thinking straight."

"Yes," Owen said. He sought his blankets and left Lawton staring at the fire.

Day after day, the two forces rode toward the

border, Geronimo following behind Lawton's command. Lawton fretted over that. "He could slip away any time he wants. The same thing happened to Crook."

Owen's nerves were wearing thin. He knew, he had been with Crook when it happened before. "What do you want to do?" he demanded fiercely. "Disarm and surround him? All you can do is act as though you trust him." Again, he got Lawton's reluctant agreement, but he knew the same old argument would come up again in the morning.

Couriers left and arrived steadily at Lawton's camps. Miles was being informed of every step.

"Has Miles left yet?" Owen kept asking.

Lawton winced. "He demands that I accept Geronimo's surrender. The general hasn't moved yet."

Owen swore passionately. "What the hell is he trying to do? Geronimo was promised he could talk to him. Do we break another promise? Is Miles afraid to meet with him?"

An agony of embarrassment was in Lawton's eyes. "He demands an absolute guarantee that Geronimo intends to surrender. If he gets that assurance, then he will come down."

Owen's face flushed with passion. "What's he trying to do? Make sure that what happened to Crook can't happen to him?"

The vehemence of Owen's outbreak startled Lawton, but he said nothing.

"Christ almighty," Owen exploded. He wished he could wash his hands of the entire matter. He was sick and tired of assuring Geronimo each day that the Big Chief was coming. Each time he told him that, he was sure suspicions grew in Geronimo's eyes.

"You tell the general that success or failure is in his hands," he said hotly. "If he doesn't want to bother to meet Geronimo, then let him say so. What happens after that isn't your fault. Let Geronimo believe that we're all liars."

His impassioned denunciation seemed to brace Lawton. "We arrive at Skeleton Canyon tomorrow. I'll wire the general he must see Geronimo there, or take full responsibility." He looked calmer, and his jaw was set.

"Good," Owen snapped. If that didn't get Miles off his ass, nothing would.

They arrived at Skeleton the following day. Before evening arrived, Lawton showed Owen the reply. "Miles sounds like he's unhappy," Lawton said and grinned. "He's on his way by wagon. He should be here in two or three days."

"I hope that satisfies Geronimo," Owen said in disgust. If Miles didn't arrive soon, Owen fully expected to awaken some morning and learn that Geronimo had slipped away in the night.

He spent as much time as he could in Geronimo's camp, trying to keep up with Geronimo's changing moods. Geronimo knew what he was doing, but he said testily, "I will wait until the Big Chief arrives." He bent a glowering look on Owen. "But he must come soon."

Miles arrived three days later. Owen rode into Geronimo's camp to notify him.

Geronimo grumbled, "Do not tell me. The Big Chief finally consented to talk to me. Gray Fox would not have treated me like this."

Owen groaned inwardly. If Miles met Geronimo with pompous airs and Geronimo matched it with truculence, the chance for a constructive peace talk would be blown skyhigh.

"He is a very busy man," Owen said desperately.

"Gray Fox was never that busy," Geronimo observed. "I was all his business." A faint smile touched his face. "I promise you that I will not go into the meeting angry." He waved his hand at the nearby squaws and children. "I am thinking of them." He cackled at the relief showing on Owen's face. "You will take part in the talk?"

"If I'm needed, Geronimo." Owen spoke quickly to erase the scowl on Geronimo's face. "I am only a minor chieftain. Do your minor chieftains take a big part in your important talks?"

Geronimo considered that, then laughed. "Only as much as I want them to."

Owen echoed the laugh. “Our people are no different.”

He took Geronimo back to Miles’s camp, and the general stepped out of his tent. He moved quickly forward to Geronimo, his hand extended. “I am glad to see you.”

Owen sighed as he stepped back. He couldn’t criticize Miles’s behavior. Miles treated Geronimo with every respect, every courtesy.

Owen remained on the fringe of the talk. A few times, Miles looked at him and frowned. Owen moved slowly away. His job was completed; he had brought Geronimo in. He thought sardonically, this is Miles’s big moment. He doesn’t appreciate others sharing it.

The talk lasted all that day and into the next. Several times, Geronimo gesticulated fiercely. No anger reflected on Miles’s face.

Geronimo finally stood, shook hands with Miles, then turned toward his camp.

Owen hurried to catch up with him. He caught the infinite sadness in Geronimo’s manner. His shoulders slumped and his eyes were dull. “It is done,” he said. “I must go to Florida. Perhaps it is for the best I long to see my wives and children.” He looked squarely at Owen. “I do not expect to see you again.”

“Maybe you will,” Owen said. A thought occurred to him, and he asked, “You will not break your promise, like you did with Gray Fox?”

"I did not break a promise," Geronimo said indignantly. "Gray Fox broke his."

Owen's face darkened. "Not once did he ever—"

"He did, when he was bringing me back into Arizona."

Owen looked astonished. "Where did you get that idea?"

"From Tribollet. You know him?" At Owen's nod, Geronimo went on. "He sold us whisky. He told me that we would be killed as soon as we crossed the border. If we were not all killed, we would be taken to Florida."

"No," Owen said appalled. "Gray Fox never had any such thoughts for you and your people."

"Tribollet said he did," Geronimo said flatly.

Owen's face hardened. His job wasn't quite completed. He would get the truth out of Tribollet, even if he had to knock it out of him.

"Something troubles you," Geronimo said, his curiosity showing.

"Nothing I can't handle," Owen growled.

He mounted and looked down at Geronimo. "I wish you happy days."

Geronimo nodded acknowledgment. When Owen looked back, Geronimo was still standing there.

Owen found Miles surrounded by members of his staff. Miles's high good spirits showed as he accepted their congratulations. A squadron of troopers was now surrounding Geronimo's camp, and the collection of his weapons was just beginning.

Owen stopped a moment and stared at Miles. This Miles looked more like the one Owen had first seen, confident to the point of cockiness, pompous boasting showing on his face and in his words.

"Gentlemen, it took long and hard planning to force Geronimo to surrender. But when he found out he was against a stronger and more clever hand—" Miles paused and laughed modestly. "Why, there was nothing else for him to do."

Owen felt a sickening disgust rise in his throat. Miles was milking his moment of glory for all he could get. From his words and manner, one would think he had accomplished the mission all alone. Owen thought of Lawton and of all the other men who had suffered. He thought of Crawford and Grimes and the other dead. Passion darkened his face. Goddamn it, he had a small hand in this surrender.

Owen choked down his irritation and was able to smile. He no longer needed the glory moments that were so necessary to Miles.

Owen pushed through the officers around Miles. Miles looked up and saw him, and his jaw sagged perceptibly. He flushed, and his lips tightened before he said crisply, "What is it, Lieutenant?"

Owen wondered with sardonic amusement what would happen if he denounced Miles's grab for glory. All the others here would be stunned, and perhaps they would denounce him, for the glory trail was still important to them. It didn't matter. Each one would probably know that Owen's denunciation was true, but they would give him no support.

For a moment, Owen felt nostalgia grip him and freeze his tongue.

"Speak up, speak up," Miles said impatiently. Those shrewd eyes never left Owen's face. He was apprehensive of anything Owen might say.

"I wanted to tell you, General, that I'm resigning my commission."

Owen heard the harsh, audible sucks of breath all around him. Shock registered on Miles's face, then he grabbed at this opportunity offered him.

"I'm sorry, Lieutenant," he said smoothly. "But I wouldn't attempt to dissuade you. I've always said each man knows what's best for him."

Miles impatiently returned Owen's salute, eager to get back to his self-praise. He no longer had a rival who might attempt to grab a share of the limelight. Lawton would know the truth, but he still rode the glory trail, and that efficiently muffled him.

Owen looked at all the officers eager to share Miles's great moment. He shook his head, but the old disgust didn't return. What they did or how they did it no longer mattered. He wanted to throw back his head and laugh in uproarious delight. It had been a long time since he had felt so free.

# Chapter 19

Owen saw evidence on every street corner that the news of Geronimo's surrender had reached Tucson. Men whooped in sheer exuberance and mauled each other in an excess of high spirits, released from the pall of dread that had threatened their very existence: a lonely ranch no longer need fear the approach of another night, a wagon or mule train could set out with every expectation of making its destination. It was small wonder that people were celebrating. Long before nightfall, Tucson would be a drunken city.

Owen was sorely tempted to see Stella right away, but he had something to do first. As great as the temptation was, it would have to wait.

He dismounted before Tribollet's saloon. It was too early in the morning to expect customers, but he thought he might find Tribollet here, preparing for another day's business.

The saloon was empty except for the lone bartender, who listlessly wiped the bar. He recognized Owen from that long-ago fight that had smashed up the saloon, and his face stiffened. Then he forced a sour smile as he said, "I guess we owe you a drink for the job Miles did in bringing Geronimo in." He reached for a bottle. "That was sure more than Crook could do."

Owen waved the offer aside. The bartender had it all wrong, just as most of Tucson would have it. Already, Miles was reaping the sole credit.

Owen smothered the stab of resentment. This was something he was going to have to get used to.

"I want to see Tribollet," he said mildly.

The bartender studied him, then decided there was no menace in Owen. "Too early for him. I doubt if he's up. You might find him in his hotel." He gave Owen directions.

Owen nodded his thanks and wheeled and walked toward the door. He looked back and saw the bartender eyeing him speculatively. Owen smiled grimly. It was a good thing the bartender didn't know what he had on his mind.

He found the hotel, and the clerk listened to his request. "He hasn't come down yet. He's in room 204." The clerk was in a garrulous mood. He wasn't going to pass up the opportunity to talk to somebody in the Army.

"They finally sent somebody out here who could take care of those damned Apaches, didn't they?"

There was that stab of resentment again. Owen pressed it down. "Looks so," he agreed, and walked up the stairs.

He knocked on Tribollet's door, and a voice yelled, "It's not locked."

Owen stepped inside. Tribollet turned from the

mirror, a razor in his hand, his face half-lathered. He remembered that former meeting with Owen, and there was no forgiveness in his voice as he growled, “What do you want?”

Owen closed the door behind him. “Just a few words.” His voice was deceptively mild. “Go ahead. I’ll wait.”

Tribollet finished his shaving, wiped off the razor, and laid it down. “What’s on your mind?” he asked in a surly tone.

“You still selling whisky to the Apaches?” Owen asked.

A flash of apprehension raced through Tribollet’s eyes. “You must be out of your head. I don’t know what you’re talking about.”

Owen moved toward him. “I think you do.” His voice hardened. “Geronimo says you sold him whisky when he was coming in to surrender to Crook.”

Again, that apprehension filled Tribollet’s eyes. “Then he’s a goddamned liar,” he blustered. “I never knew an Apache who had the truth in him.” His eyes flicked to the razor.

Owen caught the look. He saw no other weapons in sight, but a razor could be a nasty one.

“Quite a few white men fit that description, too, don’t they?” he said.

Tribollet’s temper broke its leash. “Get out of here,” he yelled. “I don’t have to stand here and listen to your crackpot ideas.”

“You do, if you’re responsible for all the misery that was caused by Geronimo running again.” Owen was sure that Tribollet paled. “Why did you tell him that the Army was going to kill all the Apaches the minute they got across the border?” Owen demanded. “Or at least, take all of them to Florida?”

Tribollet breathed harder. “You’re out of your goddamned head.” His tone had a rasping note.

“I don’t think so,” Owen said. He took a long forward step, swinging as he completed the move. He hit Tribollet flush in the mouth, knocking him against the washstand. The washstand spilled over, and the pitcher and bowl crashed to the floor. Tribollet fell on them.

He stared at Owen with pain-glazed eyes, his hand fumbling for the razor.

Owen kicked the razor aside before Tribollet touched it. It slithered across the room, making a small clattering sound.

Owen bent over Tribollet. “Are you going to tell me about it, or do I have to beat it out of you?”

Tribollet glared at him with murderous eyes. “Goddamn you,” he said in a shrill voice. He struggled to regain his feet.

Owen didn’t let him fully make it before he hit him again. He tried to hit Tribollet in the same spot. He didn’t want to knock him unconscious. Tribollet crashed into the wall behind him. His legs were rubbery, and he slid to the floor, his eyes out of focus.

Owen reflectively rubbed his knuckles. He was making a hell of a lot of noise. He hoped he could finish what he came to do before somebody interrupted.

Tribollet sat on the floor, his back against the wall. He bled from the mouth and nose. He stared dazedly at Owen, shaking his head to clear it. He rubbed the back of his hand against his mouth, smearing blood all over his face.

"All you have to do is to tell me about it," Owen prodded. "You'd save yourself a lot of trouble."

Tribollet made it to his hands and knees. He remained in that position, head hanging low, his breathing harsh and labored.

Owen watched him closely. Maybe the resistance was already beaten out of Tribollet, but Owen didn't think so.

He saw the bunching of Tribollet's shoulder muscles and heard the animal-like growl. Tribollet launched himself from his hands and knees, his arms spread wide to sweep Owen's legs from under him.

Owen stepped inside those spread arms and met Tribollet's dive with a sharply raised knee. He caught Tribollet full in the face. The brutal impact lifted and knocked him backwards. Tribollet landed on his back. His eyes rolled up into his head. He shuddered and was still.

Owen swore softly. He didn't want Tribollet unconscious. He needed water to revive him, and the pitcher was shattered.

He kneeled over Tribollet's chest and slapped him methodically with first one hand, then the other. Tribollet's head rocked back and forth.

Owen made the successive blows harder. The pain was getting through to Tribollet. He groaned several times, and his hands rose to ward off the punishment.

He opened his eyes and stared unseeingly at Owen.

Owen straightened and stood over him. "Do you want to tell me about it now? This can go on for a long time."

A shuddering sob wracked Tribollet. His breathing bubbled the blood on his mouth.

Owen drove his boot toe into Tribollet's ribs. "I mean what I say, Tribollet."

The final slap, or the culmination of all the punishment, shattered the last of Tribollet's defiance. "I sold him whisky," he blubbered. "I told him those things."

Owen felt limp and bruised. It had to be the strain, for he hadn't been physically hurt except for the bruising of his knuckles.

"What are you going to do with me?" Tribollet whimpered.

Owen's eyes were filled with loathing. For a few dollars' profit, Tribollet had prolonged the horror of the Apache war. There was a long, black score against Tribollet's name. Owen thought of the murdered victims in lonely ranchhouses, unsuspecting teamsters surprised on the trail, and yes, the soldiers who had died trying to corral Geronimo. That didn't include the struggle and hardships of men in uniform, or all the horses and mules ruined, or the blanket of terror that Tribollet had laid over the country. And all for a few dollars' profit. Owen resisted the impulse to kick Tribollet again.

"I'm going to turn you over to the Army," he said matter-of-factly. "I think the Army will call it treason and stand you before a firing squad."

Tribollet squalled in pure terror. "I did it, but it wasn't my idea. I was paid to do it."

The announcement startled Owen, though he should have realized Tribollet didn't have enough brain power to think of such a plan.

"I'm not going to take all the blame," Tribollet went on in a shaky voice.

Owen breathed slowly and carefully. "Who paid you?"

"Mundane," Tribollet blurted out. "Captain Mundane. He paid me two hundred dollars. He told me what to say to Geronimo."

The name sent a wave of nausea through Owen. He might have accused Mundane of many things, but not this: not this traitorous behavior to his uniform, to his country, and its people.

"Why?" He had to control his voice to get the question out.

"He didn't want the war against Geronimo to end. If it did, all the fat profits from the Army contracts would stop."

The sickness increased in Owen until he thought he would vomit.

"Don't you see?" Tribollet pleaded. "I had to do what he said. He's my boss. He owns most of the saloon."

"Get up," Owen said harshly. His rage returned at Tribollet's cowering, and he reached for him.

Tribollet shrank back from those hands. "What are you going to do with me?"

"You may save your life by telling the Army just what you told me. That depends upon how an Army board sees it. You're going to ride out to Fort Lowell with me." He unsnapped the flap of his holster. "Or I'll blow out your brains here. Either way, it doesn't matter to me."

That could be a flash of hope in Tribollet's eyes. Owen squashed it. "If you've got any idea of calling to anybody when we get outside, forget it. I'll be happy to tell everybody in Tucson what you did. They may hate Geronimo, but they'll hate you more for turning Geronimo loose again." His tone was almost reflective as he went on. "I'd say they'll hang you. If some of them are crazy enough to try to save you, I'll shoot you on the spot."

Tribollet's hope faded. He struggled to his feet. "I'll go," he said feebly. He knew what the people of Tucson would do to him if they learned of his complicity. He didn't know what the Army would do. It was easier to accept the unknown against the positive reality of the known.

Tribollet shuffled through the door with Owen right behind him. Tribollet threw out a hand several times in going down the stairs to bolster his wobbly legs.

The clerk was wide-eyed as he saw Tribollet's bloody face. "What happened?" he asked in horror.

"Just a little accident," Owen said easily. "I'm taking him where he'll get the proper attention."

The clerk didn't fully believe Owen's explanation, but he made no further protest. The wide-eyed stare followed Owen and Tribollet all the way to the door.

Owen made a decision before he reached his horse. Tribollet said his horse was in Likens's livery stable, several blocks away. It would take time to reach it, plus the danger of running into people who could be foolish enough to intervene in Tribollet's behalf.

"Get up." Owen motioned toward the horse.

Tribollet didn't understand him. "There's only one horse," he faltered.

"I can see," Owen said grimly. "We're riding double. If you try to make a break before I mount, I'll blow you out of the saddle."

He waited until Tribollet was seated, then vaulted up behind him. Riding double would make an uncomfortable trip to Fort Lowell, but it wouldn't kill either of them.

# Chapter 20

The sentry at Fort Lowell was bug-eyed as he saw the doubly-burdened horse approach. He looked at Tribollet's slumped-over figure, at his bloody face, and his mouth slowly opened.

"Don't worry about it, soldier," Owen said and grinned. "You just let Colonel Lindell do the worrying."

Nodding to the sentry, Owen kicked his horse into motion again. He grinned sardonically as he thought of how the sentry's mouth had sagged. That sentry would have something to talk about tonight.

He pulled up before headquarters and jumped to the ground. He jerked Tribollet out of the saddle and shoved him toward the door. Tribollet was really scared now. The fear and the pain of his broken features were contorting his face. Spittle ran from his mouth, mixing with the blood. He wasn't a pretty sight.

"If you want to save your ass, you tell the colonel exactly what you told me," Owen said. "If you get cute on me, I swear to God, I'll take you out and turn you over to some of the ranchers who lost their families in Apache raids."

Tribollet looked at him with fear-sick eyes. He had no intention of trying to be cute.

The corporal in the outer office had the same reaction as the sentry.

"It's all right, Corporal," Owen soothed him. "The colonel is expecting us."

He shoved Tribollet toward the inner door. He looked back and grinned. The corporal's mouth was hanging open a foot.

Colonel Lindell's head snapped up from his work at their entrance. His eyes widened. Maybe the colonel's reaction wasn't as extreme as the sentry's and the corporal's, but it showed.

"What the hell—" Lindell started.

Owen shoved Tribollet down into a chair. "This man has a story I think will interest you, Colonel. Go ahead," he said to Tribollet.

Tribollet sat with hanging head, his hands dangling between his knees. For a moment, Owen thought Tribollet either didn't hear, or didn't understand him. He gripped Tribollet's shoulder hard.

Tribollet looked up at him with agonized eyes, drew a shuddering sigh, then began talking in a dull, almost inaudible voice. He told Lindell exactly what he had told Owen in the hotel room.

Lindell's eyes grew more bleak as he listened. He jerked visibly as though he had been struck when Tribollet spoke of Captain Mundane's part in this.

"My God," he said with repugnance. He looked at Owen as though seeking confirmation.

Owen nodded slowly.

"You swear to this?" Lindell asked Tribollet when he finished.

"He'll swear to it," Owen said. "He knows he has no other way to go."

Tribollet nodded reluctant assent. He looked like a man spent after a long run.

Lindell stood and shouted, "Corporal."

The corporal came into the room at a run. Experience had taught him how to react to that tone.

Lindell didn't even give him time to ask what the colonel wanted. "Call the officer of the guard," Lindell ordered. He stabbed a finger at Tribollet. "I want this man put under arrest."

Lindell sat down and waited grim-faced, his fingers drumming on his desk while he waited for the guard.

Lieutenant Sims looked questioningly at Lindell, then at Owen and Tribollet. Unanswered questions flooded up into his eyes, but he wisely held them.

"Lock this man up, Lieutenant," Lindell barked. "Charges will be made out immediately. I want him kept under the closest guard. You understand that?"

Sims caught the unmistakable threat in Lindell's voice. "I do, sir."

"Get him out of here," Lindell said, the loathing strong in his voice.

"Come on," Sims said roughly, as he took hold of Tribollet's arm and pulled him to his feet. He didn't know what this man had done, but from the expressions on the colonel's and Owen's faces, it was bad.

Tribollet's movements were those of an old, infinitely weary man. He didn't look at Owen as he stumbled out of the room ahead of Sims.

Lindell waited until the echo of footsteps faded. He looked at Owen, and he was pale. "My God," he said, his breathing making an odd, whistling sound. "This is unbelievable."

"It is," Owen gravely agreed.

Lindell reached into a desk drawer and pulled out a bottle of whisky. He placed two glasses beside it.

"I need a drink," he said huskily. "I think you could stand one, too."

"I could, Colonel."

Lindell filled both glasses. He handed one to Owen and drank his in a single gulp. He poured another for himself and offered the bottle to Owen.

Owen held up his half-filled glass. "This one is holding out, Colonel."

Lindell shuddered as he finished his second drink. Owen had seen many men shudder after a stiff drink, but Lindell's reaction wasn't to the whisky.

"It's unbelievable," Lindell repeated. "It makes you feel like you need a bath."

"Yes," Owen said simply, and let it go at that. He couldn't say it any better.

"Do you think your man is telling the truth?"

"He is," Owen replied. "We had quite a discussion before he wanted to tell me about it. You saw his face."

Lindell looked curiously at him. "How did you get wind of his involvement?"

"Geronimo told me about Tribollet. Tribollet's lies were the reason Geronimo broke his promise to General Crook. He believed Tribollet."

Lindell crashed his fist against his desk. "All that misery prolonged because of those lies. That man deserves hanging."

Lindell hadn't mentioned Mundane. Owen felt uneasy about that. Was Lindell trying to protect Mundane? If so, there could be several reasons—Mundane was a fellow officer, and his father was a senator. Did they motivate Lindell, or was it just an abhorrence of the shame that was bound to come?

"I told him he might be stood up before a firing squad and shot for treason," Owen said.

Lindell's eyes had a hard, brilliant shine. "You called it right, Lieutenant. Treason is the correct word. I'm going to use it in my charges against Captain Mundane."

Owen blew out a relieved breath. Lindell wasn't

avoiding anything. "Colonel, I was afraid—" His hands raised and fell helplessly, and he didn't finish.

"That I would try to protect Captain Mundane?" A flicker of a smile touched Lindell's lips. "Perhaps because of his father?"

"Something like that," Owen confessed.

Lindell shook his head in disgust. "If he was the president's son, it would make no difference. A man hates to get his hands soiled in such filth."

Owen nodded. Lindell had a neat way of putting things. "There's one thing I'd like to ask, Colonel. I'd like to bring Mundane in."

Lindell eyed him speculatively, then nodded. "You've earned that, Lieutenant. Do you know where his quarters are?"

Owen shook his head, and Lindell gave him directions.

"You don't think you'll need help?" Lindell asked.

"No help," Owen said flatly.

"I think the charges will be ready when you return, Lieutenant."

"Yes, sir," Owen replied and walked out of the room.

# Chapter 21

An officer lounged on the porch of the officers' quarters, and Owen asked further directions of him.

"The third door down," the officer responded. "Neal's there. I saw him go in not five minutes ago."

Owen nodded his thanks and moved on. The officer showed no curiosity now. That would change when he learned the reason Owen was here.

He stopped before the door of Mundane's quarters to be sure his rage was under control. When he saw Mundane, he knew he would want to break him into pieces with his hands. He drew another deep breath. He could safely look at Mundane now.

He threw open the door and stepped inside. Mundane, stripped to his undershirt and drawers, lay on his cot. His fingers were laced behind his head, and a self-satisfied expression was on his face as he looked at the ceiling. That look wouldn't last long, Owen thought coldly.

Mundane raised his head at the sound of Owen's entrance.

"Hello, Neal," Owen said. There was no real greeting in his tone. His face was an immobile mask, his eyes as hard as stone.

Mundane sat up, an angry flush mottling his face. "What the hell do you think you're doing? Who told you to come busting in here like this?"

A faint, sardonic smile moved Owen's lips. "Nobody, Neal. But I thought you'd like to hear the news." He saw the holstered pistol on the washstand beyond Mundane's cot.

Mundane swung his feet to the floor, growing visibly angrier. But he was curious enough to ask, "What news?"

"Bob Tribollet's on the post. I just brought him in."

That put an uneasiness in Mundane's face. He tried to meet Owen's eyes and couldn't. "Why should that interest me?"

"It should. Colonel Lindell put him under arrest. For treason."

Mundane's Adam's-apple bobbed convulsively, and color ebbed from his stiffening cheeks. His eyes shifted from Owen's. He licked his lips as he tried to digest what Owen said.

He stood, but there was no menace in the motion. He struck Owen as a badly harassed man, looking for a place to hide.

Mundane made an effort to speak, and the words stuck in his throat. He tried again, and his voice was a hoarse croak. "I don't see where that concerns me."

"It should," Owen repeated. "You paid him two hundred dollars to lie to Geronimo when he was coming in with Crook. You kept the war with Geronimo going on."

Mundane looked as though the bottom of his stomach had dropped out. His eyes were glazed, and his hands trembled. He tried to laugh, and it was a strained, unnatural sound.

"Why should I do that? Everybody knows Tribollet's a damned liar. Who'd believe him?"

"Colonel Lindell does. I think an Army court will believe him, too."

Mundane's face was the color of rain-soaked dough. "You're crazy," he said hoarsely. "Why should I do that?"

"For a few more damned, dirty dollars," Owen said savagely. "Tribollet told the colonel you owned most of his saloon. Your interest went beyond that. It won't be hard to prove you were part of the Tucson Ring. As long as Geronimo didn't surrender, the fat contracts with the Army would go on." He remembered how friendly Mundane and Ulman had seemed the night he saw them together at the cockfights. "I think Ulman will gladly tell the court just how much interest you had in his business. Once he feels a little pressure, he'll only be concerned with saving his own hide."

The shot struck home, for Mundane visibly blanched. "Lies," he said shrilly. "You can't prove anything."

Owen's restraint broke, and he lashed Mundane

with every invective at his command. He couldn't get the verbal whipping out fast enough. "You know damned well a court will prove everything. I wouldn't want to be in your boots when you face that court. Every officer on that court will want to spit on you. You're filth, Mundane, and they'll know some of that filth will rub off on them just having to listen to you. You broke every vow you made—to yourself, your uniform, your country. Your defense lawyer will be sickened just to sit next to you. He'll put up a poor defense for you. He won't have had any experience in defending treason."

Mundane's face was ashen, and he looked as though his legs wouldn't support him. He kept shaking his head, mumbling over and over, "No, no."

Owen went on relentlessly. He painted a vivid picture of the contempt Mundane would face. "I think you'll be shot for treason. The court won't be able to arrive at any other verdict."

Mundane looked as though every bone in his body had melted. His eyes were closed, and his lips kept moving, but only a moaning came from them. The sound was made by a mortally wounded animal.

"And your father," Owen went on. "Think of the proud senator. He's pulled a lot of strings for you, hasn't he? He won't be able to find any strings to pull now. I doubt if he'll even want to.

He'll feel like everybody else does. He'll disclaim you."

Owen was suddenly infinitely weary. He stopped, not because there was nothing more to say—he hadn't begun to get the loathing out of his system—but because Mundane was so spiritually whipped that he probably no longer heard Owen.

He shook his head in utter distaste. "I don't see how you're going to face it, Mundane. I know I couldn't. If I was in your place, I wouldn't face it. I'd use that pistol on the washstand."

Mundane's head snapped up, and his eyes held a crazed glitter.

Owen was suddenly sick of this whole mess. "Get dressed! I guess your uniform can stand a little more debasement. I'll wait outside for you."

He thought surely Mundane would say something to that. But Mundane just stared at him with that odd intensity.

"I'll give you five minutes," Owen said. He strode to the door, opened it, and slammed it behind him. He stood on braced legs, staring blankly ahead. Everything seemed normal out here. The officer lounging on the porch glanced casually at Owen. Two soldiers passed by, one of them laughing at something the other said. In the distance, Owen heard the barked commands of a drill instructor. Nothing was normal in the room behind him. Owen thought of the moments he had just spent in there and spat to rid himself of an unbearably foul taste.

The glory trail had broken so many men. Names ran through Owen's mind—Crawford, Grimes, Crook . . . It seemed there came a time when the glory trail demanded a harsh, stiff price as toll for having traveled along it. Did every man have to pay that toll? He couldn't say about General Miles. The trail hadn't yet presented its bill to Miles. But it would come. With absolute conviction Owen knew that no man escaped paying that toll.

He whirled about as the shot sounded in Mundane's room. For an instant, he was held motionless, not in shock, nor even surprise. With what Mundane faced, how could he go any other way?

The shot pulled the lounging officer to his feet. He ran toward Owen, reaching him just as Owen stretched a hand toward the door.

"Did I hear a shot?" the officer asked, his voice tight.

"You did," Owen said crisply. He opened the door but didn't step inside.

Mundane lay face down on the floor, his pistol a little way from his outstretched hand. The trickle of blood from his head steadily increased.

Owen looked at Mundane with somber eyes. A tiny shiver ran through him as he thought of those tortured last moments Mundane spent.

Mundane hadn't dressed. Had the enormity of what he did reached him so that he couldn't bear to don his disgraced uniform once more? That would be giving Mundane more credit than he deserved, Owen thought. The probable truth was that Mundane couldn't face what lay ahead of him.

"Good God," the officer gasped. "Neal shot himself."

"Yes," Owen said the obvious.

The officer turned an agonized face toward him. "But why?"

Owen shrugged. "I guess only Neal knows that."

The officer started to push by him, and Owen's outflung arm stopped him from entering the room. "You can't do anything for him," he said with brutal honesty. "You'd better go get a doctor. I'll report it to Colonel Lindell."

The officer's face was heavy with stupefaction as Owen left him. He wouldn't be satisfied with the sketchy explanation Owen had given him, and he would probably pull and twist at the happening for many days. When the news got out, the entire post would ask the same puzzled questions. Only Owen and Lindell would know the answers. Owen knew he wouldn't talk of it, and he was quite sure Lindell wouldn't, either. Tribollet might, in a frantic effort to save himself, but that didn't matter. He doubted Tribollet's story would be given much credence, now that Mundane was dead.

Lindell frowned as Owen walked into his office alone. "Where's Captain Mundane? Didn't you find him?"

"I saw and talked to him," Owen said tersely.

Some dread touched Lindell's eyes at the harsh, clipped tone. "What happened?"

"He shot himself, Colonel." Owen made no attempt to soften the announcement.

Lindell's lips pressed together in a tight, bloodless line, and he stared at his clenched hands. Then he sighed, and his mouth and hands relaxed. "You saw it?"

Owen shook his head. "I waited outside his door for him to dress." More explanations were useless.

"I guess he couldn't face the disgrace," Lindell muttered.

"That's about as close as we'll ever come," Owen said.

"It's best for everybody," Lindell said. He looked fiercely at Owen as though he dared him to criticize his words.

Owen nodded somberly. He knew what Lindell meant. The shame Mundane heaped upon the Army would never come to light now. Owen didn't know or care how it would be handled. If he was interested in making a guess, he would say Mundane's death was due to an unfortunate accident. He imagined that the official report would say that Captain Mundane was killed while cleaning his pistol. He agreed with Lindell's summation. This way would be best for everybody concerned.

"Colonel, I have to turn my horse in to the Army."

Lindell stared at him puzzled.

"But I want to ride back to Tucson. I'll leave him at Likens's stable. Will you have somebody pick him up?"

"But why?" Lindell asked.

"I resigned my commission to General Miles some days ago. I had one other thing to do before I made it official."

Lindell didn't argue with Owen's reasons; or perhaps in a vague way he understood. "I'm sorry to hear that, Owen." He sounded much older and suddenly very tired. "But you know best."

"Yes," Owen said. Routine bound a man with nearly unbreakable chains. His hand was halfway to his head before he caught the motion and lowered it. He didn't have to salute anybody; he was no longer in the Army.

He turned to go, and Lindell checked him. "Good luck," he said softly. "The Army will be forever grateful to you, even though it may not fully know why."

"Yes, sir," Owen said, and walked toward the door.

# Chapter 22

Owen left the horse at Likens's with instructions that the Army would pick it up.

Likens was an old man with a wrinkled, crafty face. "This puts you afoot, Lieutenant," he said with sly humor.

Owen laughed. "For a while."

Likens had a keen nose for a business opportunity, and he tried to sell Owen a horse.

"Not now," Owen declined. "Maybe I'll see you later." He doubted that. He had never known a professional horse-trader that didn't have a dishonest streak in him. They seemed to get more pleasure out of tricking prospective customers than from the purchase price. When Owen bought a horse, it wouldn't be here.

As he walked toward the Tydings house, he thought soberly that buying a horse would sorely stretch the money he had. He was going to have to find something to do, in a hurry. He felt strangely unfettered and at a loss. Routine might be a shackle, but taking it away left a man uncomfortable.

He knocked on Stella's door and waited. His heart picked up that familiar rapid beat. He had known Stella many months, but the actual time he had spent with her was pitifully small. Now, he could spend all the time he wanted with her. But would she want him to? He felt painfully inadequate, and the question scared him.

Stella opened the door and stared at him speechless.

Owen gravely looked at her. "Hello, Stella," he said huskily.

Her hand went to her throat, and those magnificent eyes were round in wonder. "Owen." She seemed to have trouble saying his name, for it sounded weak and shaky. "Owen," she repeated, and this time her voice was stronger.

She squealed with delight and sprang toward him, her arms wrapping about his neck. If he had any doubts about her feelings toward him, the ardor of her greeting dissipated them.

She covered his face with kisses and managed to gasp, "It's been such a long time."

He held her face between his hands. "But you knew I'd come back."

She met his steady gaze unflinchingly. "I could only hope. But so many days passed."

"I know," he said before he kissed her. He lifted his head and looked into her eyes. "I love you."

"It took you long enough to say it." Mock grumbling filled her voice.

He was filled with awe as he realized what she was telling him. "Stella, does that mean you love me, too?"

She nodded without looking at him.

He shook her gently. "Why didn't you tell me?"

The question put an indignant flash in her eyes. "Did you expect me to say it first?"

He smiled at the spark in her. "I guess not," he admitted. "How long have you felt like this?"

"For ages," she said airily. "I was beginning to despair you'd ever find your tongue."

"But Mundane was always around," he fumbled. "How could I know?"

She regarded him sternly, then sighed. "I kept him around for one reason: to prod you. But you were so slow. I was beginning to believe you'd never learn."

He laughed with newfound assurance. "But I have now." He tried to pull her to him again, and a rosy blush spread over her cheeks. "If we stay out here much longer, Father will come to see what happened to me." She tugged on Owen's hand. "He'll be anxious to talk to you again."

This time, he didn't follow her down the hallway. He couldn't; she wouldn't let go of his hand.

Tydings rose as Owen entered the courtyard, and his eyes shone with pleasure. He held out his hand.

Owen raised his hand. Stella still held it. "I can't shake hands with you," he said and smiled. "She won't let go of me."

"Ah," Tydings said softly. He looked from his daughter's face to Owen's face and nodded in hearty approval.

"Will you let go of him long enough for him to sit down, Stella?" Tydings asked.

Stella sat on the arm of Owen's chair, a hand resting on his shoulder.

"The last we heard of you, you'd gone out to talk to Geronimo," Tydings said. "Then all reports stopped. We couldn't get word from anybody about what was actually going on."

"I can imagine," Owen said soberly. "I talked to him."

Tydings's keen perception showed. "Then it was you who convinced him to surrender?"

Owen laughed as he remembered how Miles had taken over everything, once he knew it was all set.

"Did you hear differently?"

"All Tucson is talking about General Miles's handling of that savage."

Owen caught the tinge of distaste in Tydings's voice.

"But you don't accept that?"

"I do not," Tydings said promptly. "I have seen General Miles twice. He struck me as a vain, glory-seeking man."

Owen nodded. "He's different from Crook," he said, and let it go at that.

"But that's wrong to let him take the credit," Stella said indignantly.

Owen squeezed her hand. "It's not important anymore. But what is important was that I found out why Geronimo bolted on General Crook." He debated about telling them everything, and decided he should. These were the people closest to him, and he could get all this off his chest. It wouldn't stop him from thinking about it later, but it would minimize the burden.

"Geronimo told me Bob Tribollet sold him whisky and told him that he would be killed by the Army, or shipped off to Florida. He did the only thing left to him. He ran."

"How awful," Stella breathed.

Tydings watched Owen with rapt attention.

"It was worse than that," Owen said slowly. "Somebody paid Tribollet and told him what to say."

Her eyes flashed. "I hope you can find that man."

Owen turned in his chair so he could squarely face her. "I did. Neal Mundane was behind it all. He owned most of Tribollet's saloon and had an interest in the Tucson Ring. He didn't want to see the campaign against Geronimo stopped. That would end most of the contracts the Ring had with the Army."

Owen watched Stella closely. She had known Neal Mundane well. If that shocked her, he couldn't tell. Perhaps her breathing was a little faster.

"I'm not surprised," she said evenly. "Poor Neal. All he talked about was the money he could make in Tucson. He was obsessed with the subject. I still say he should be arrested."

"I tried to," Owen said simply. "He couldn't face the disgrace. He shot himself."

He heard the startled intake of her breath. She briefly closed her eyes. When she reopened them, a sheen of tears glistened in them. "Poor Neal," she said again. "But maybe it was best for him."

Owen let the tension ebb away. She showed the normal amount of grief, no more. Any sensitive person would have done the same.

"It stopped an ugly mess from being made public," Owen said. He hesitated before he dropped his last bomb. "I resigned my commission. You're looking at a man out of a job."

Both Stella and her father startled. "Why?" Stella demanded. "Because of Neal?"

Owen shook his head. "No." He thought he saw a knowledge in Tydings's eyes. "And not because of Miles, either." He made a vague gesture. "There comes a time when a man has to change his road." Someday, he might give them a fuller explanation, but not now.

"What will you do?" Tydings asked.

Owen smiled faintly. "I'm not sure. I haven't put too much thought into it yet. I'd like to go into ranching. I know horses and stock. If I move quickly enough, maybe I can pick up one of these abandoned ranches cheap." He was silent with thought. With the Apache menace gone, all those ranches would be quickly snapped up.

"Who am I kidding?" he said roughly. The brutal candor was directed at himself. "I couldn't scrape up even a down payment."

Stella and Tydings exchanged glances, and there was some kind of agreement in that exchange.

"Would you consider staying in Arizona?" Tydings asked.

"I know the country," Owen said. He cursed the bad timing of everything. Just when he found Stella, he was empty-handed.

"I have to live in Arizona," Tydings said. "Stella and I have often talked about it. But I have to have something to do. I have a little money saved, and Stella's mother left her some money. Together, we can buy any ranch you choose. We could be partners."

"No," Owen said violently. He was half angered at the proposal. The violence went out of his voice. "I wouldn't be bringing anything to such a partnership."

"Only the knowhow," Tydings said in a gentle derision. "Only what is needed to make a success of it." He stood and said, "I've noticed before he's a stubborn man. Talk some sense into him, Stella."

Tydings smiled and walked into the house.

"I wouldn't consider it," Owen said stubbornly. "What kind of a man do you think I am? What—"

Stella leaned over and stopped his words with a kiss. “A smart one, I hope.”

“No,” he said. “I—”

Again, she stopped further words by kissing him. “Do you think I’m going to let you get away after all this time?”

He opened his mouth to protest more, and she kissed him. “I can keep this up all night,” she warned.

His chuckle grew into a full laugh. “How can I stand up against such an indomitable will? I give up.”

“You’d better keep that in mind,” she said, before her lips touched his again.

**Center Point Large Print**
600 Brooks Road / PO Box 1
Thorndike, ME 04986-0001 USA

**(207) 568-3717**

**US & Canada:**
**1 800 929-9108**
**www.centerpointlargeprint.com**